Praise for
KRISTINE KATHRYN RUSCH'S
DIVING UNIVERSE

The Diving Universe
(Reading Order)

Diving into the Wreck: A Diving Novel

The Application of Hope: A Diving Universe Novella

Becalmed: A Diving Universe Novella

City of Ruins: A Diving Novel

Boneyards: A Diving Novel

Skirmishes: A Diving Novel

The Falls: A Diving Universe Novel

The Runabout: A Diving Novel

Searching for the Fleet: A Diving Novel

The Renegat: A Diving Universe Novel

The Spires of Denon: A Diving Universe Novella

Escaping Amnthra: A Diving Universe Novella

ESCAPING AMNTHRA

A DIVING UNIVERSE NOVELLA

KRISTINE KATHRYN RUSCH

*wmg*PUBLISHING

Escaping Amnthra

Published 2020 by WMG Publishing
www.wmgpublishing.com
First published in *Asimov's SF Magazine,* Sept/Oct 2019
Cover art copyright © Philcold
Book and cover design copyright © 2020 by WMG Publishing
Cover design by Allyson Longueira/WMG Publishing
ISBN-13: 978-1-56146-242-1
ISBN-10: 1-56146-242-X

ESCAPING AMNTHRA

AMNTHRA

A DIVING UNIVERSE NOVELLA

Raina Serpell never asked for this. Any of it.

She was the de facto captain of the *Renegat*. She had no leadership training, no engineering training, no knowledge of ships. Her training—decades ago—had been as a linguist, and that had been a job she completely adored.

Except that it brought her here—to the bridge of an SC-class vessel with way too little crew, on its way home from the most disastrous mission in Fleet history.

The captain was dead, the engineers most likely dead, half the people who knew anything about this ship completely gone, and a good quarter of the crew she had had been injured in a battle for control of the ship that had gone so poorly, a good number of people had died.

And she needed all of them right now, because the *Renegat* was under attack.

"Is there any way to strengthen the shields?" she asked the bridge crew in general.

The bridge crew wasn't really a crew so much as a group of inexperienced survivors who managed to cobble together a journey on a ship they didn't really understand.

The bridge showed it. It was filthy because there was no discipline. Cups were scattered everywhere. Some food stains lingered on the side of a console near her. No one wore uniforms, and no one had an assigned station.

The only person with any kind of engineering experience was Yusef Kabac, and he had been fired from his last engineering post nearly a decade before. He had arrived on the *Renegat* as a navigator, and he'd been asked (forced) to leave that post as well, by the now-deceased captain.

She sat in the captain's chair. It was too large for her small frame, so she always had to sit with her back straight, and feet above the floor. She felt like a child when she sat in it, an unworthy child.

But she sat anyway because it was the best way to use the tools of this SC-class vessel—even though she didn't know how most of them worked.

No one else did either. Serpell didn't trust Kabac's knowledge, but at least he had some. She also didn't trust him. He stood near the navigation controls—his old station—and kept glancing at the *anacapa* drive. The drive enabled the *Renegat* to travel long distances through foldspace—something someone had once explained to her as a shortcut that the drive achieved by folding space, the way one would fold a blanket.

She had no idea if that was right; she had no idea if any of this was right, but she didn't have time to think about right at the moment.

Something on the planet beneath them was actually shooting at them. They were stuck in orbit—how, she did not know—and they couldn't seem to pull out of the trajectory they were on.

She was trying everything she knew, which was almost exactly nothing, and none of it was working.

"Anyone?" she asked. "Shields?"

Everyone—all eight of the others—looked at Kabac, like they always did when Serpell had a technical question. Kabac's skin reddened beneath the black beard he'd been growing since the Captain Preemas demoted him, all those months ago.

"I don't know," he snapped. "Shields aren't my specialty."

"Is anything your specialty?" Gajra Blaquer snapped back. She sat on a stool near the console directly behind Serpell. Blaquer was so short that she had to sit on something so that she could reach the controls easily. "I mean, you keep saying you don't know anything about the *anacapa* drive, and then you say *I have no idea* half the time we ask you a technical question, and—"

"Gajra," Serpell said tiredly. "This isn't doing us any good."

Blaquer shut up. Serpell didn't have to turn around to know that Blaquer was glaring at both her and Kabac. Blaquer hated authority—all authority, even authority she had chosen herself, as she had done here.

The ship rocked as something hit it—probably some other kind of shot. Although Serpell didn't know where it would have come from. The shots they'd received so far had only come from one part of the planet below them, and they were on the other side of the planet at the moment.

If only they could break out of this orbit. She'd tried everything she could think of. She'd tried forcing more power into the engines. She'd tried commanding the ship to power its way to other coordinates. She'd set the automatic pilot and put more coordinates into the ship.

None of that seemed to work.

She was thinking about using the *anacapa* drive, but she didn't know if she could do that in this forced orbit, so close to a planet.

Although she did know that sector bases had *anacapa* drives, and sector bases were located on planets.

Usually deep underneath planets, though. The Fleet engineers who had designed the sector bases had put them underground for a reason, and she was terrified that the reason was because using an *anacapa* drive aboveground on a planet would cause some kind of problem.

She didn't know that, though. She didn't know anything, really, and that scared her. She'd been asking Kabac, but Blaquer was right: Kabac didn't seem to know anything either.

Serpell put a hand over her face. She was so tired and so terrified and so out of her depth. Every day brought a fresh new horror.

This one, though, she had stumbled into herself.

She had listened to this ragtag crew, and she shouldn't have. She should have trusted her own instincts.

Even though her instincts were telling her to go to her cabin, lock the door, and climb into bed, never to get out again. She didn't want to see any of this. She didn't want to make any more decisions. She didn't even know how to think tactically.

In fact, tactical thinking confused the heck out of her. How the captains of the Fleet thought in three dimensions and looked out at the scenarios around them, and thought about how to fix everything while keeping all the disparate personalities that were the crew in place, she had no idea.

She couldn't even multitask on the bridge. She had shut off the screens because she didn't want to see how big the planet was in comparison to them, how the weapons fire actually showed up as it came from some point below, something through the haze of clouds that encircled the planet.

"I thought there was a space station," Declan Connelly said with such typical obtuseness that Serpell wanted to yell at him to remain quiet.

Of course there was a space station—if you could call some big construction in orbit of a planet a "space" station. The thing was inhabited too—or it seemed to be—and all of the troubles began when Serpell told Marquis Iaruba to hail that station with a nonstandard help-us message.

All she wanted was more supplies, and the nonstandard message had said that. Instead, the ship got fired on or grabbed or something. Whatever it had been had hurled the ship into this orbit.

And then—Serpell believed—the ship was locked into this orbit by whatever. Because she couldn't get the ship out of it.

Although part of her believed that any pilot or captain or anyone who actually knew what they were doing would be able to get the ship out of orbit in a heartbeat. She was terrified (that word again) that she had gotten the *Renegat* into a standard orbit herself, and she was too stupid to get it out.

"We're not going to hit the space station," she said, controlling her voice. She hadn't told everyone that the orbit the weapon had tossed them into was above the orbit for the station, but she figured they would have known that. After all, it had initially shown up on the image on the screen to their right—the two-dimensional image showing a flat planet and lines around it that represented orbits.

She had shut that screen off first because it had irritated her the most. The planet wasn't flat, and the orbits didn't disappear behind it. But the one thing that that particular image had shown was the one spot on the planet where all of the weaponry was firing from.

The *Renegat* had about twenty-two minutes before they crossed within range again.

The first two times the *Renegat* had gone over that area had proven disastrous. The first time, the weaponry pulled them into this orbit; and the second time, something different had hit them with great precision, not quite getting through the shield.

She knew how to do some rough calculations, and those calculations told her that if they got hit again by that same weapon at the same intensity, the shields would be gone.

"I would rather shoot the hell out of that weapons station as we near it than do anything with the shields."

The tense voice behind Serpell made her close her eyes in exasperation. That voice belonged to her wife, India Romano. India, who insisted on being on the bridge, even though she had no technical skills at all.

She had been a linguist just like Serpell, only she hadn't been a good linguist. India hated the work, calling it tedious. She had always done a haphazard job, although she'd been pretty good at interpreting. She could read people's expressions as well as their words. Her interpretations had never been word-for-word accurate, but they'd always been close enough.

Everything India had done had been close enough. And that had screwed her with the Fleet over time. Then she'd been placed on this ship, and Serpell had gone with her rather than staying behind—the stupidest decision of Serpell's life, aside from marrying India in the first place. Once on board this ship, Captain Preemas had seen something in India, and made her security—with no training at all.

India had defended him, nearly to the death, and if that hadn't been bad enough, she was the one who had started all the shooting after the engineers murdered the captain. She was the one who had gotten more than twelve people killed all by herself.

"Of course you would want to do that," Serpell said, keeping her voice dry. But she could hear the thread of irritation running through it anyway. "Shooting is the answer for you, isn't it?"

Everyone within Serpell's line of sight grew tense. She supposed the crew members behind her had grown tense as well. Working with her and India probably hadn't been pleasant for any of them. It certainly wasn't pleasant for Serpell.

"You should give me more credit," India said. "Without me, you wouldn't be heading home right now."

"Without you, we wouldn't be at this godforsaken planet," Serpell snapped. India seemed intent on undercutting her in any way possible. And that included riling up the rest of the crew. They had been worried about getting stuck in foldspace. They had been worried that their supplies wouldn't hold, particularly if they got stuck for a year or more.

Serpell had done the math for them, over and over and over again, but it hadn't assuaged them. For some reason, most of them couldn't grasp the fact that with half of the crew gone, the food would stretch twice as long.

India wanted to stop for supplies and so India scared them with the getting-stuck-in-foldspace talk and here they were, being shot at by some locals on some planet they didn't even know the name of just because they were asking for food they really didn't need.

"You blame me whenever you make a bad decision," India said.

Serpell whirled, and as she did, Jane Zerpa reached out from the console nearest to the captain's chair, and caught Serpell's arm.

"Not now," Zerpa said, gripping hard.

Serpell shook her off, which was difficult, since Zerpa outweighed her by at least fifty pounds. Somehow Zerpa gained mass and muscle in the past few months, probably because she didn't want to get caught physically between two opposing factions again.

Serpell ignored her, even though she knew Zerpa was right. This wasn't the time. So Serpell wouldn't take a lot of time. But she needed India to shut up.

Her gaze met India's. India's eyes and hair always matched, even now, as the ship was on limited resources. Right now, India's eyes were bright kelly green, which looked just fine. But the kelly green in her hair made her look like her skull had been overtaken by some kind of plant from the hydroponics bay.

Serpell couldn't remember why she had ever found India attractive, or why she believed she had loved her enough to give up her entire life for her. India had killed not only the feelings, but the memory of those feelings with almost every single word she had spoken since Captain Preemas had died.

"If you can't contribute in a positive way," Serpell said, her voice vibrating with anger, "get off my bridge."

Zerpa froze beside her. Blaquer glanced at Connelly. No one else moved. They were all staring at either India or Serpell.

"Your bridge, is it?" India asked.

"No one else is taking point," Serpell said. "And it's too late now. You're distracting us. Get the hell out of here."

"You need me," India said.

She wasn't going to leave. She wanted to fight instead of save the *Renegat*. Which was just typical. India never thought things through. If she had thought things through, they wouldn't be on this ship in the first place.

If she had thought things through, she would have known that firing laser pistols in an enclosed space at a fortified door would have been bad for the people firing, not for the people behind that door.

That was why Serpell was the most furious. India had killed people through her own stupidity and wouldn't even acknowledge what she had done wrong.

"I don't think we need you, India," Blaquer said with that same dry voice she had used earlier.

"I think even if we did need you, India, you're a distraction." Hari Kellman's deep voice echoed across the bridge. He was a round man who somehow disappeared into the walls—and he liked his anonymity, so the fact that he spoke at all showed how disturbed this confrontation made him.

"You should leave," Zerpa said forcefully.

"Hear that, Raina?" India said. "You're dividing the crew. You know that doesn't work—"

"You should leave, India," Zerpa said. "Just get out of here. You're trouble no matter where you go."

India turned her head slightly, as if she couldn't believe someone had spoken to her like that. And then she let out a small snort, making her disbelief both clear and audible.

"If you think I'm the problem," she said, "then you people deserve whatever you get."

She stood slowly, and strode toward the exit, as if leaving a scene. Such an idiot.

Serpell shook her head slightly. She felt like a woman who had taken some kind of hallucinogenic drug, and could barely remember the high through the worst hangover of her life.

"Shields," Serpell said as she slowly turned back toward her chair. "Anyone have ideas about the shields?"

"I've been studying them," Kabac said, as if he were the newest person to the bridge crew, as if he hadn't been the only one of the group who had *ever* served on a bridge crew, "and I think they're at maximum."

"That's not what I've found," Kellman said. "With your permission, Raina, I'll do what I can to bolster them."

Serpell wished this crew didn't ask permission. They made it about her, when she knew as much as they did.

"Sure," she said, because if she didn't, they wouldn't do anything at all, and everyone would die. "Bolster away."

She was going to see if she could get the automated weapons system to work. Technically, they needed a captain or some ranking officer to activate the weapons, but they didn't have one.

She had looked at the system before, back when they started on this journey, and she had tried to familiarize herself with the workings of the *Renegat*. She had read Captain Preemas's logs, both the ones he had planned to turn into the Fleet when he returned (or maybe he had just sent that information to the Fleet) and the ones he had put together for himself or for some other kind of glory. (She never pretended to understand Captain Preemas.)

The private logs continually discussed the need for the weapons system to work, for a captain to understand it, and for a captain to make it work all by himself. Captain Preemas had been worried that something was going to happen to the ship when they arrived at the Scrapheap, which had been the point of their mission.

Things had happened at the Scrapheap, but not what anyone expected.

Shortly after the *Renegat* had arrived at the Scrapheap, the engineers had mutinied against Captain Preemas, and India had gotten a number of people killed.

Serpell shuddered, just remembering that.

But she kept it all firmly in mind throughout the journey so far, including Preemas's paranoia about weapons. She had studied the weapons system as much as she could, but she had never practiced with it.

And she had been too scared to try any of the virtual tests of the system. Since they had no engineers on board, they couldn't fix anything if something went wrong.

She had to sit properly in the captain's chair, and that took some wriggling to figure out. The weapons array was invisible to anyone else besides the captain, and that had to be by design.

She had never seen Captain Preemas in this chair, but then, she hadn't been on the bridge much at all while he was captain. She had stumbled into this job, partly because she was trying to prevent India from taking it.

Serpell had made yet another mistake when she let India and the others who had fought with Captain Preemas out of the brig. The engineers and their supporters were gone, and Serpell had thought that she could deal with India and the others. She had thought they'd be grateful to be freed.

Instead, they felt betrayed by everyone. And India announced her intention to run the ship.

Serpell had trotted after her, trying to prevent disaster. By the time she realized that India didn't have the stomach for all the work it would take to be captain, it was too late: people were already deferring to Serpell, because they knew she was so much smarter than India.

India had said she didn't care, but she did. She had sat in the back of the bridge and made her snide comments—when she could be bothered to come to the bridge.

But Serpell had been careful not to let India see the weapons system. Or any of the defensive equipment. Because Serpell was afraid of what kind of use India would put it all to.

But now that India was off the bridge, Serpell was a little more comfortable opening up the weapons system. As far as she could tell, it only worked as a holographic screen. There was no way to activate it from the consoles.

She didn't understand that design, but she suspected, from something she had seen in Captain Preemas's logs, that he had deleted easy weapons access as the ship devolved into factions. He didn't want the engineers to control the weaponry, so he removed it from their sight.

From everyone's sight.

Serpell had to sit precisely in the center of the captain's chair to activate the weapons system. It created a shaded three-dimensional screen, something that blocked her view of the bridge before her.

She had done this only once before, late one night when no one was on the bridge. (The fact that no one else was on the bridge was something she didn't know how to fix. Someone should always be on the bridge, but she couldn't seem to assign someone to guard the bridge and have that assignment stick. How did captains do anything?) That night, it had taken her nearly an hour to convince the system that she was the acting captain.

Fortunately someone had registered Preemas's death, so the system knew he was gone. And neither of the former first officers were on the ship, nor were any of the officers who had been in line for the captain's position in a standard ship.

So after the system had searched for someone with real authority, it actually took her identification and accepted her. She wasn't sure if she was grateful that Captain Preemas hadn't entered everyone's new rank when he had thrown out the Fleet's rank structure on the ship or if she hated him for it. Because if he had changed the structure in the computer, then this stupid orbit, this being trapped above the stupid planet they couldn't name, this situation they were in—it would be someone else's problem.

But it wasn't. It was hers.

And the ship had given her permission to operate this system. She just wasn't sure exactly how to do it.

She did learn how to activate the voice command and synch it to her voice. She could even subvocalize, which she had been afraid to set up because she tended to mutter.

Her heart was pounding as she stared at the weapons system. It still looked overly complicated, with words and numbers and information she didn't understand at all scrolling down one side. Trajectories and targets and distances and possible materials and possible weapons—

The entire thing made her vision blur, and her brain hurt. She was not ready for this.

So instead, she looked at the weapon system's three-dimensional map. It showed the entire solar system and the placement of Fleet vessels in that system. Theirs was the only ship with an actual Fleet signature.

The *Renegat* looked lonely in its orbit around the unnamed planet.

Fleet ships were automatically exempt from the weapons system. She had discovered something in Captain Preemas's notes that said she could alter that, but she didn't want to. And she wasn't exactly sure why the man had wanted to fire on Fleet vessels anyway.

Not that it mattered. She had to force herself to focus.

Serpell didn't even know the name of this solar system. Neither did Justine Breaux, some kind of historian or something, whom Captain Preemas had relied on to tell them if they had ended up in the right place after a foldspace journey. Breaux was below decks right now, still trying to figure out if this planet had once housed a sector base.

Because that would explain the weapons system. It seemed to be firing at them from an uninhabited part of the planet, on top of some really large mountain ranges. There were five continents, one really large—where the fire was coming from—and four smaller ones, along with some islands scattered throughout.

Only the readings showed no human life on the large continent and lots of it on the islands and smaller continents.

No one was answering their hails from those places, though. No one was communicating with them.

Breaux believed that if there had been a sector base here, it would have been on the large continent, because the Fleet showed a penchant for building its sector bases under mountain ranges.

More than once on this entire trip, Serpell had cursed the Fleet's habit of losing its history. Everyone had. Because the *Renegat* had been going backwards through systems, traveling back to places where the Fleet had been, sometimes thousands of years before. The Fleet never went backwards. The order to send a ship back to an old system the Fleet had abandoned was just the first strange thing about this journey.

There had been so many others, long before Serpell took over the ship, that she couldn't even keep track of them all in her own head.

She had stopped trying.

At least this solar system was familiar to her.

Serpell had studied all of the systems they found themselves in when they came out of foldspace. The Fleet divided its travel space into sectors, although she'd never been able to figure out the rhyme nor reason behind those sectors. It seemed to her that they were designations based on how far the ships could easily travel without activating the *anacapa* drives, and as the ships got more efficient, the sectors themselves became bigger.

The last two had encompassed at least four or five hundred solar systems, which made the sectors so big that Serpell's mind could barely handle them.

But she had dutifully looked at them, looked at where—long ago—the Fleet had established sector bases, and searched for the people who were the descendants of the Fleet, still living on those planets.

When the *Renegat* was deciding who to ask for help, they couldn't find any indication of where the sector base had been. That wasn't unusual. Only twice had they found the later sector bases.

This sector, if it followed the usual pattern, should have housed Sector Base N, but the *Renegat* had no information on that base. And she wasn't sure where it had been.

She guessed, based on the space station, that it had been here. But Blaquer had pointed out the flaw in Serpell's logic—much too late, of course.

Um, y'know, Raina, space-faring people travel, *right? Just because a space station is here, doesn't mean that the Fleet built a base on this planet.*

Yeah, good. Very helpful. No one was being helpful, and now they were all being shot at.

Serpell hadn't brought the *Renegat* here to have the entire ship destroyed. Not after everything the ship and this so-called crew had been through.

The weapons system was extremely complicated, with commands that used codes, mostly, probably to prevent some amateur like her from accessing it.

She didn't want to poke around the system—she couldn't poke around the system—but she did want to try one thing.

She tapped the holoimage in front of her, activating the voice system. The command for subvocalization came up almost immediately, and this time, she tapped it.

She was going to keep tight control of her own mouth, making sure she didn't speak out loud unless she needed to.

At that thought, she raised her head above the weapons system, saw her crew (*her* crew?) scattered across the bridge. Everyone was working, heads bent, except Kabac (of course) whose gaze met hers.

She mouthed, *Get to work.*

He glared at her, then bowed his head like a sullen child.

She sank back into the captain's chair, and swallowed hard. Speaking softly but forcefully was going to be interesting, but she would do it.

First, she needed to see what she was up against.

"Shields," she said slowly.

And immediately, information popped onto the right side of her three-dimensional screen. The *Renegat*, surrounded by a clear yellow light.

Shields.

She almost laughed out loud. She hadn't finished her initial command. The system had anticipated her and brought up the image of the *Renegat's* shields. She was going to ask if the planet had some planetary system of shields or if the shields were haphazardly placed around only the most important installations on the planet itself.

She had spoken so slowly that she had caused the misunderstanding. Good lesson to learn right at the start. Imagine learning it in the middle of some battle somewhere.

"Increase shields to full," she said, not even sure "full" was a command.

The shield around the *Renegat's* image changed from yellow to bright red.

More numbers ran across the screen below.

"Change commands to simple commands," she said. "No numbers. Just words."

The system winked out for a half second—long enough to make her panic. Then it blinked back on with words—labels!—everywhere.

And below the image of the *Renegat* was a warning scroll: *Shields can maintain full strength for seven days only.*

She let out a nervous laugh, one she couldn't stifle.

If they were still here seven days from now, they were screwed. Or dead. Or something.

She wouldn't need seven days.

She hoped.

"Hey!" Kabac said. "Something happened to the shields!"

"I didn't do it," Kellman said. "I was trying, but I didn't manage it."

"My controls say they're on full," said Iaruba.

"We can't do that forever," Blaquer said.

"We won't," Serpell said out loud, then glanced at the system, terrified she had screwed something up because she had spoken normally. But nothing had changed.

Apparently subvocalizing meant subvocalizing.

"I found the controls," she added. She wanted to say, *Now shut up and let me work,* but she didn't because she wasn't sure if the system would take that as a command to do it.

She hated testing this in the field. She hated using this system at all.

"We have taken fire from the planet below," she subvocalized to the system. "Can you locate the source of the attack?"

Two areas lit up—and, weirdly, they had names. In fact, the planet had a name. It was labeled Amnthra on this system. She wanted to ask where the names came from but she didn't dare. She didn't know exactly how far away they were from that spot on the planet—Amnthra—where the weapons' fire had originated from, but she knew they were running out of time.

The shots were coming from a mountain peak on the big continent, which was the one without the people as far as she could tell.

Then there was another area near the space station where some kind of beam was coming from.

If the shots were coming off the planet, then that beam was the thing holding them in orbit.

First things first. She had to get rid of that weapon on the planet.

"Show me the planetary defenses," she said.

Nothing changed. She wasn't sure exactly what that meant. Maybe there were no planetary defenses.

"Show me defenses around—" she peered at the name on that mountain range "—Denon."

There was a bubble, but surprisingly, it didn't protect whatever was shooting. It protected the valley below.

If she had to guess, she would think that maybe the sector base had been down there, and someone had left the old initial defense system on top of the mountain range. But wouldn't that have registered as Fleet tech?

She couldn't think about that right now. She couldn't think about any of it.

She glanced to her left, and realized she had been completely ignoring that part of the weapons system. It showed the entire planet, and the *Renegat* herself, which was getting dangerously close to those shots.

She was running out of time. She couldn't think and choose and decide what to do. She couldn't learn this system, unless she wanted to risk the *Renegat* getting hit all over again.

Sure, the shields were on full at the moment, but she wasn't sure if that would be enough to stop whatever they were lobbing at the ship.

"Okay," she subvocalized, her mouth dry. "Destroy that weapons system on the planet's surface, on the place marked Denon. Fire at will."

She added that last only because she had once heard another of her captains (years ago) say the same thing.

The weapons system flashed green at her twice—an acknowledgement?—and then built a target around the entire mountain top and that shielded valley.

Really? That large an area? Seriously? What if there were people down there? What if they were doing something—

It didn't matter, she didn't have time to find out, they were trying to destroy the *Renegat* after all, and everyone on board the ship would die if those people below succeeded, and it was her duty to make sure the ship was all right—

And, at that moment, the *Renegat* shuddered ever so slightly. The little image of the *Renegat* showed a barrage of images released from different parts of the ship—some from the nose, some from the back, a few from the sides and a lot from underneath.

Everything the *Renegat* unleashed went straight down to the planet, heading for that mountain.

"What did you do?" Kabac demanded.

But she didn't answer. Somehow her hands were over her mouth. She didn't remember putting them there. The weapons seemed to take forever to cut through the atmosphere and get down to that mountain range but when they did, that entire part of the continent lit up.

Someone swore behind her. And then someone else yelled—but she couldn't tell if it was with joy or anger or fear.

"Hey," Zerpa said, "something's happening on that space station."

"Yeah," Kabac said. "You obliterated whatever that was down there. They're going to retaliate."

They were, weren't they? Whoever they were. They were going to attack the *Renegat* if they had other weaponry. And right now, the *Renegat* was in orbit around the planet, an orbit the space station seemed to control.

"System," Serpell subvocalized, not sure if she should use the word *system*, but she did anyway. "Cut off that beam by any means necessary."

She touched the image of the beam, just to make sure the system knew what she was talking about.

The system highlighted the space station itself. She drew in a deep breath, not sure if she should stop the order—after all, people were on there. People who hadn't responded to her emergency hails. People who had fired on her.

But…people nonetheless.

Although she didn't know that for certain.

All of those thoughts ran through her head in a split second, and as they were going through her head, the same barrage of weapons released from the *Renegat* again, this time heading directly for the station.

It blew up—spectacularly—debris going in all directions.

"Get the *Renegat* out of this orbit!" she shouted, but she wasn't sure who she was shouting to. The weapons system wouldn't accept shouting—she thought anyway—and Kabac wasn't really acting as navigator.

But right before her, on the three-dimensional screen, she saw the *Renegat* turn slowly and pull itself out of the orbit.

Someone (something?) had listened to her.

"You did it!" Kellman said.

"Yeah, and it looks like she got someone's attention," Connelly said. "I'm getting notifications that ships are powering up all over the planet below."

"We gotta get out of here," Serpell said.

"If what I'm reading is right," Blaquer said, "those ships can follow us all over the sector. And since you used most of our weapons to obliterate part of their planet, they're not going to let us go."

"We're going to have to use the *anacapa* drive," Kabac said, and Serpell was afraid he was right.

Had she used most of the *Renegat's* weaponry? She had no idea. She didn't know they had limited weapons. Someone should have mentioned that.

"How far are we from the next foldspace entry point?" she asked. It was a general question. Everyone had been tracking where they had initially come out of foldspace and where they were going into it, trying to rebuild the same route they had gone on when they traveled to the Scrapheap, back when Captain Preemas was still alive.

"Far enough," Kabac said.

"Not that far," Kellman said at the same time. "We can get there if we leave right now."

"If those ships don't chase us," Blaquer said.

"Even if they do," Zerpa said.

Serpell stared at the weapons system, arrayed in front of her. There was a smoking crater on the planet below, where there had been a mountain peak not fifteen minutes ago. A smoking crater.

Somehow she hadn't expected the weapons system's images to show actual smoke. But, she supposed, if it was that visible, it must have been horrible on the ground.

Bile rose in her throat. A smoking crater.

That system on the planet had better have been automated.

She made herself nod. It had to have been automated. If there were people—

They had probably been under that dome shield in the valley.

She swallowed hard, keeping the bile down. The *Renegat* wasn't out of this yet.

The space station was gone too, and the people on the planet below were going to want to retaliate. Those ships were activating.

Serpell made herself focus. "How many ships are there?" she asked.

"God," Iaruba said. "A hundred at least, from various launch points. It's as if every city on that planet is launching vessels at us."

Why would a planet have such great defenses against a space attack? Did they have major enemies somewhere? Was that why they never answered the hails?

Serpell wiped her hands on her thighs, leaving sweat marks on her pants. She was starting to shake.

She couldn't shake. She didn't dare lose it.

They weren't done.

"Get us to that foldspace launch point," she said to Kabac or whoever was going get them there. "And fast."

She turned and looked at Kellman as she said that. He was nodding. He, at least, was trying to be competent. Kabac wasn't even trying sometimes.

"Yusef," she said to Kabac, "be ready to launch us into foldspace."

Then her breath caught. She was giving orders out loud. Fortunately, she was doing so full voice. But sometimes she muttered. She hadn't muttered, had she?

"I'm not sure the *anacapa* drive has had enough rest," Kabac said.

"And what about getting extra supplies?" Blaquer said.

"We can wait," Iaruba said, sparing Serpell the need to answer.

They could wait.

"What are you going to do?" Blaquer said. "We don't have enough weapons to hold them off."

Blaquer couldn't know that for certain, because Serpell didn't know that for certain. The weapons system wasn't saying that anything was low.

Of course, she wasn't sure what she had fired at them. She wasn't sure what was available, either. Some of it couldn't be materiel. Some of it had to be lasers, and those didn't run out, did they?

She had no idea.

She adjusted one of the controls on the system, hand shaking because she still didn't know what she was doing, and saw the ships that Iaruba had been talking about. They had powered up, but they still hadn't left the planet's atmosphere.

And Iaruba had been right: there were at least 100, maybe more. Most of them were small fighters. There was nothing, as far as she could see, that was as big as the *Renegat*.

That was good on the use-of-force side, but bad on the maneuverability side. Smaller ships could get closer faster.

"System," she subvocalized, "target all non-Fleet vessels. Don't let them get near us."

The lights of the targeting system illuminated more ships than she had originally seen, all of them in a strange greenish glow. But the *Renegat* didn't fire on any of them, and she realized that her orders were too vague.

"Destroy each ship," she subvocalized. Then she thought about what Blaquer said about the limited weapons resources. "But don't use more weapons than necessary."

She wasn't sure if that would work. She wasn't sure if any of it would work.

If the ship got too close, then the *Renegat* would have to go into foldspace early—that was all there was to it.

The *Renegat* started firing—nothing as dramatic as the sheer firepower it had lobbed at that mountain peak and the space station. Just a shot here and there, mostly destroying ships trying to come out of the atmosphere close to the *Renegat*.

"You should wait until they get into space," Blaquer said. "Because that debris is going to fall all over that planet and kill lots of people."

Serpell pretended she didn't hear that. She couldn't hear it. She didn't want to hear it, not ever.

And she wasn't going to answer Blaquer. Serpell didn't dare. If she spoke with the wrong tone, then she might give the weapons system the wrong commands. She was barely managing to handle the system as it was.

She reached up a hand to shut down the weapons systems screens, and then decided against it. What if, when she did that, the entire system shut down? What if it deleted her orders, thinking she had vacated them or something?

She had no idea if that was what was going to happen, but she had to think it might.

So she swallowed hard again, and fairly shouted at Kabac. "Make sure we can get into foldspace at any point."

"It doesn't work that way," he said.

"Well, make it work that way," she snapped.

She didn't have to see him to know that he was shaking his head. He infuriated her. Not as much as India, but close.

"Hari," Serpell said, deciding to act like a captain for the first time in her life, "back him up on that, will you?"

She had no idea if Kellman could back anyone up on the *anacapa* drive, but she did know that he was 100 times more competent than Kabac. If there was a way to figure out how to make the drive work or how to get into foldspace right away, Kellman would find it.

She hoped.

The weapons system was picking off ships that came out of the atmosphere near the *Renegat*. Serpell was trying to look at all of this as a game of some kind, not thinking of the ships filled with people.

Of course, they had to be soldiers, right? And soldiers signed up for things like dying in battle, right?

She swallowed hard, but let the system continue to shoot as the *Renegat* sped toward the coordinates that someone—she had no idea whom—deemed the best to get them into foldspace out of this sector.

So far, none of those ships had made it off the planet's surface.

And then she realized that her assumption about the ships had been wrong. None of the ships near the part of the planet she had initially shot up (they! They had shot up! The *Renegat* had shot up) had made it out of the atmosphere. But others were coming around from a part of the planet she hadn't been watching.

Dozens of ships, flying in some kind of formation, and they all started shooting at once.

Immediately, the shield grid on the weapons system lit up, both as the shots collided, and then with warnings.

Shields losing integrity, the first warning said.

Then was immediately followed by *Shields readjusting to repel weapons fire*. And something blurred along the edges of her three-dimensional screens.

"Raina," Zerpa said, her voice shaking. "They have weapons designed to get through our shields."

"I'm seeing that," Serpell said. "The system is adjusting."

"So are their weapons," Zerpa said.

And the system confirmed it. Another *Shields losing integrity* warning appeared, followed by a *Shields readjusting* notification.

"You have that on automatic, don't you?" Kabac shouted.

Serpell wasn't sure why he was shouting, or if he really needed to shout or if shouting was important at all.

"Of course," she snapped, having had enough of him. "What do you think I am, a weapons expert?"

"If so, what you're doing is predictable," Kabac shouted.

So is what you're doing, she nearly shouted back. *You're not working on the* anacapa *drive.*

Instead, she managed to hold onto her temper, at least verbally, and say, "Just get us ready to go into foldspace."

"If we go in while they're shooting at us, they might hit the drive and do real damage," Kabac said.

Excuses. This man never thought of anything except covering up what he couldn't do.

"Yeah," she said, "and if we stay here, we get destroyed. *Get us out of here.*"

"Now?" Kellman, not Kabac, asked.

Serpell frowned at the weapons system. The shots from those ships weren't just getting through the shields, they were doing real damage to the exterior of the *Renegat.*

She didn't have anyone who could fix the exterior of the ship—or any part of the ship for that matter.

"Yes, now!" she said.

They had to get out of here, and it didn't matter how.

Because she didn't know what she was doing with those shields. The weapons system was still picking off the ships, one at a time. Apparently, those ships didn't have shields that would block shots from the *Renegat*, although it seemed like those ships didn't have shields at all.

Why would someone design fighter ships without shields?

She didn't want to think about it. If she thought about it, she would make more things up, as in maybe the ships were automated or something.

A shudder ran through the entire *Renegat*. Her weapons display whited out for a half second, and then rebooted. Or reappeared. Or re-somethinged.

If the fighters took out the weapons system, she was really screwed. The *Renegat* was really screwed.

They would all die.

"Why haven't we entered foldspace?" she asked.

"It's not that easy—" Kabac started, but Kellman interrupted him.

"We're almost to the coordinates we need," Kellman said. "I'll activate the *anacapa* in three minutes."

Three minutes might as well be three hours.

"It's not ready," Kabac said, loud enough for everyone to hear.

Serpell peered over the weapons display. Kellman was beside Kabac, working on the same console. Kellman was blocking Kabac with his body, keeping them slightly apart, as if he no longer trusted Kabac.

Maybe no one trusted Kabac.

Another shudder went through the *Renegat*. This time, the weapons display didn't white out. It remained. But on the larger holographic image of the *Renegat*, a red hole appeared on the starboard side, near one of the cargo bays.

Then a warning light appeared: *Hull breach on Deck Four. Shield destroyed.*

Apparently, not the entire shield, but part of the shield, the part near the cargo bay.

"Get us out of here!" Serpell repeated. Then she sub-vocalized, "Fix shield near the cargo bay."

But nothing happened on that command. Nothing at all.

"Okay, we're there," Kellman said. "I'm sending us into foldspace."

"We need a shipwide announcement," Kabac said. "People need to brace themselves."

More shots were fired around the *Renegat*, missing somehow, at least according to the display.

Then the *Renegat* shuddered. It bumped as if it were physically on a road and hit ruts.

Serpell had gone into and out of foldspace more than a dozen times now, and she had never felt anything like that before. Some of the entries had been scary rough, but not like this. She had to grab the edge of the captain's chair just to hold herself in place.

Whatever was causing the bumping got deeper, almost as if they were going into deep ruts, or maybe even holes in a road—even though there was no road in space and no turbulence, no air pockets, nothing that would cause a feeling like this, ever.

She had no idea what it was, and she was scared to look at everyone else on the bridge, in case they were as terrified as she was. Their terror would only amplify her own.

The weapons display remained, but the solar system was gone. There was a lot of nothing where it had been, just blackness and the occasional dot, which she really did not understand.

However, the image of the *Renegat* remained on the left side of the display, and instead of one red-marked hole, there were three. And the shields were flashing a sickly yellowish-black.

There was a lot of information scrolling along the side of the display sections, but not numbers. Words. Some, in red, were warnings—the shield was at one-quarter power, or completely gone in some places. The hull had been breached in all three of those places, but so far, the ship had sealed the breach, and was wondering if someone would authorize the nanobits to fix it, and how.

But other parts were simply information, and they were scrolling in bright white—the weapons system was off-line, as it always was in foldspace. (Who knew?) Once they arrived, the system would ask her if it needed to reboot and continue its targeting of the Amnthran ships. (Who knew they had a name, as well? How had the system come up with that? Did it make that up from the ancient name of the planet? How come she didn't know?)

The system also informed her that if the fighting was done, someone had to handle the weapons array, and re-adjust any systems that got hit by enemy fire.

Yeah, right. As if that was going to happen.

She made herself focus on the words on display before her, because the bumping was really upsetting her. The words made it feel as if the bumping was just some-thing she had to get through, something the system felt was normal.

She knew, deep down, that the system didn't feel anything. She also knew just how ridiculous it was that she, of all people, was in charge, because she knew less about this ship—about *any* ship—than the automated systems did.

But she was still here, still clinging to the captain's chair, still trying to figure out what to do, even though her head bobbed and her neck wobbled and her spine felt jolted with each rut in that make-believe road.

And then the bumping stopped.

It just stopped.

The *Renegat* was moving smoothly again. A new so-lar system appeared on the weapon's array, which star-tled her. She hadn't expected a new solar system, but of course there would be, since they were in a new sector.

She swallowed, realized that she was tasting blood, realized that she had bitten part of her cheek and hadn't even noticed. She swallowed again, tongue playing with that broken part of her cheek, as she tried to concentrate.

None of the small ships had traveled with them. They seemed to be far away from the attack.

"Are we where we're supposed to be?" she asked.

She had never seen any of these sectors before. On the way to the Scrapheap, she had been in the linguistics area. Even when Captain Preemas had messed with rank and jobs, Serpell had stayed in linguistics. She hadn't wanted to move.

"I don't know if we're at the coordinates the Fleet wanted us to hit," Iaruba said, "but we're in the right sector. I recognize it. It has that weird triple moon planet not too far from here."

"We're in the right place," Kellman said. "Exactly the right coordinates."

"We were lucky," Kabac said. "We did it all wrong."

Serpell rubbed her forehead. "Well," she said, "we're here. So we did something right."

But there was a lot of damage. Stupid damage that wouldn't have happened if they hadn't gone to that Amnthra planet in the first place.

If she had trusted her own instincts, everything would have been fine.

She reached a shaking hand to the weapons array. She looked at the three damaged parts of the hull. The seals in the front and back of the ship merely covered a small section of the hull, and nothing in that part of the ship had been isolated. The system had—essentially— patched holes.

But near cargo bay on Deck Four, the system had isolated an entire section of the corridor and the area beyond.

Serpell scrolled and authorized the nanobits to start repairing the small holes in the front and back of the hull. But she knew better than to give the automated system approval to repair the entire area near the cargo bay.

For all she knew, the ship would simply build a wall where the greatest damage had been. If someone had been trapped in that area, then that person would be hidden behind a wall.

If she were on a normal ship, she would send someone down there to take care of everything— someone like an engineer or a first officer or someone she could trust.

But of course, she didn't have anyone like that. For all she knew, the person she would assign would go to that spot and glance at it and leave. They wouldn't even check anything properly.

"We need a damage assessment," Zerpa said.

Serpell felt a surge of irritation. Yes, they needed a damage assessment. Thank you, Jane, for stating the obvious. But what was the point of a damage assessment if no one could fix the damage?

"We might have to shut down some levels," Zerpa added gently, as if Serpell's silence meant that Serpell was stupid.

"I know," Serpell said. That was all she could manage. Because Zerpa was irritating her. They were all irritating her.

Serpell was tired of leading them, tired of doing the thinking for them. She wasn't very good at this, and she knew it, and it really angered her that none of them were any good at it either.

What had they been thinking, when they all decided to head back to the Fleet?

Oh, that's right. They hadn't been thinking. They had been reacting to all of the trauma that had occurred near the Scrapheap. They had been heading—or rather, *she* had been heading—back to somewhere normal, the only place she knew where other people—smart people—would be in charge of things. In charge of *her*.

She just wanted to go back to a universe in which she worked for someone, where they told her where to stand and where to sit and what to do.

Because the decisions she'd made on her own—from marrying India to joining the *Renegat* crew because of India, to letting everyone on this crew convince Serpell to head to Amnthra—were just plain stupid.

Serpell really wasn't cut out for any of this—and she knew it.

She was just more willing to do the task than the rest of them. And if she hadn't, she doubted anyone else would have taken up the mantel of leadership.

She had a hunch they would all be dead.

"We can't just wait," Zerpa said.

Serpell bit back the anger. She knew that. She wished the rest of them did.

She didn't answer Zerpa directly. Instead, Serpell activated the controls on the array, changed the command from subvocalization to standard. She had no idea what standard was, but she knew it wasn't loud voice commands, because those hadn't worked on the night she had tested the system.

Then she shut down the array.

Her left hand was still clinging to the edge of the captain's chair, her fingers aching because she had been holding on so tightly. She was still terrified, and for some reason, wasn't allowing herself to feel any relief at all.

"We're not stopping for any supplies," she said.

Zerpa gave her an odd sideways glance. As far as Zerpa was concerned, Serpell had clearly uttered a non sequitur.

The others looked over in surprise as well. Her gaze met theirs, and a few people looked away. All of them seemed to be on edge. A few of the faces had gone pale, probably from the journey, although what skin she could see on Kabac's face was actually greenish. He must have been feeling queasy from the bumpy ride.

"We're just going directly home," she said. "Hari, plot our course from foldspace entry point to foldspace entry point. Two days travel in between, no matter what."

"The distances aren't consistent," Kabac said. "Some of the coordinates are farther apart than others—"

"I don't care," she snapped at him. "I really don't. We made a big mistake going to that planet, and we nearly died, and the ship is damaged, and we have to fix it somehow, and we probably can't, so the best thing we can do is get home. You got that? We need real help now, and the only help we can trust is Fleet help. So either you all help me limp this ship along, or get the hell off my bridge."

Kabac rocked back on his feet. Kellman grinned just a little. Blaquer frowned. Zerpa bit her lower lip, then glanced around, almost as if she worried that the others would blame her for causing Serpell's outburst.

Serpell had caused her own outburst. She couldn't remain silent any longer when people irritated her. And she couldn't run this ship by consensus any more.

She needed to take control of it—as much as she could.

Apparently, her subconscious had been ahead of her brain on that, because this was the second time in the same day that Serpell had told people to get the hell off her bridge.

Or maybe fear was making her bold.

She slid off the captain's chair, and wiped her sweaty hands on her pants again. Then she glared at Kabac, who hadn't moved. Kellman's grin remained.

"I want a damage assessment when I get back," Serpell said.

"Where are you going?" Zerpa wasn't demanding the information: she sounded like a scared child whose mother was about to leave.

"To inspect the isolated section," Serpell said. "I'm going to see if the ship actually isolated an area or if the controls are malfunctioning."

"I don't see why you wouldn't trust the ship," Blaquer said.

Serpell gave her the same glare she had given Kabac. "Really? After all the damage we sustained, you believe that everything is working fine, including isolating the damaged areas?"

"Yes," Blaquer said, apparently not noticing Serpell's growing disgust. "That's a priority system and—"

"The hull is a priority," Serpell said. "It got damaged in three places. It no longer works right. You do understand that priority systems can get damaged and that will affect their ability to work well, right?"

Blaquer's eyes narrowed. She finally caught the sarcasm.

"You could send someone else," she said with an edge in her voice. "You are the acting captain."

"Who would I send?" Serpell asked. "You?"

Blaquer's cheeks darkened. "You could."

"I suppose I could," Serpell said. "So, what are you going to do if people are trapped in those areas?"

Blaquer's eyes grew wide. She clearly hadn't thought about anyone being trapped. And Serpell wouldn't trust Blaquer to rescue anyone, even if she had a detailed list of instructions.

"What are you going to do?" Blaquer asked.

Serpell didn't know. But she knew she would try to release them—if they had survived.

"Have you even checked for life signs?" Blaquer asked.

41

It was Serpell's turn to flush. She hadn't. She should have.

"Go ahead," she said, unwilling to admit her mistake. Let Blaquer think that Serpell was angry, not embarrassed. "You double-check me. See if there are life signs. If you find any, send someone to rescue them, okay?"

"Who would I send?" Blaquer asked.

Serpell shrugged ostentatiously. She had no idea, and she knew that Blaquer didn't either.

In fact, if Serpell found a problem, she wasn't even sure who she would be able to ask for help.

But she had to investigate. She had to see.

Blaquer continued to stare at her, as if she expected Serpell to respond verbally. But Serpell wasn't going to give her that satisfaction.

Instead, Serpell walked up the bridge to the exit, not meeting anyone else's gaze.

Her heart was pounding ridiculously hard again, because she had allowed herself to think about the possibility that someone—a bunch of someones—could be trapped in the damaged areas.

She probably should have gone back to the captain's chair and used the equipment there to check.

But she didn't. Instead, she was going to check the damage nearest the cargo bay. On the way down, she would use the elevator control panel to see if anyone was in trouble.

(And if anyone was, how come the *Renegat* herself hadn't let her acting captain know about it? Would that system—that *priority* system—be damaged too?)

She wanted to believe that—she hoped, well, actually, she *expected*—that no one on her crew would be in the areas that were damaged. Near a cargo bay? Why would anyone be there? And the far ends of the ship, mostly filled with equipment and storage? No one should have been there either.

Her crew—*her* crew. How ironic. She was thinking of them that way, just like she was thinking of it as *her* bridge. Her crew mostly stayed to the public areas, like mess halls and exercise rooms and entertainment centers. No one had even entered engineering that she knew of since the engineers all left. No one had gone into the cargo bays.

She had gone into the brig to set India and her friends free—that major mistake—and a number of the ambulatory crew had gone into the medical bay to check on the handful of people who were still too injured to get around easily.

But mostly, everyone stuck to the areas they had gone to before the crew had split into warring factions. If anyone was near the damaged areas, it would be because they had living quarters near those areas.

And she was finally getting to know the ship well enough to realize that the damaged areas weren't near any living quarters.

She still opened the panel in the elevator, and used the environmental system access to see if anyone was using resources in the damaged areas.

No one was.

Her brain told her—almost convinced her, in fact— that no one using the resources in the damaged areas meant that whoever had been there had died, not that there hadn't been people nearby.

But she wasn't convinced. She knew these people. None of them went anywhere they didn't have to.

And the ship had been under attack: she certainly didn't expect heroics from anyone, not in that circumstance.

The elevator opened onto Deck Four. The lights were dim and dark here, emergency lighting, which just made her stomach turn.

The air smelled burned. Beneath the stench of smoke, was a chemical aftertaste, something that made her eyes water.

She almost backed into the elevator.

Instead, she stepped all the way out. The doors closed beside her. She crossed the corridor to one of the command panels, opened it, and then asked the environmental system if anyone was in the damaged area.

The environmental system usually tracked the crew's whereabouts. Not by name, but by oxygen use. If system knew how many people were in a room, just by how much air was being consumed.

The system blinked red. Words scrolled across her request.

Inadequate information, they said. *The environmental system has shut down in quadrant CB4A.*

Of course. Boneheaded mistakes like this one were why she shouldn't be captain. She should have checked on the bridge.

But she wasn't exactly sure how. One of the engineers had shown her this trick on a previous posting, a decade ago. Actually figuring out where the entire crew was at any given moment using the right equipment was beyond her.

Still, she had to try. Because she didn't want to go down that dim corridor if she didn't have to.

She poked at a few systems, and didn't find anything that would clearly and obviously tell her where anyone was. She had access to a few names and identifiers—she could find India, because they had set up on the buddy system when they first joined the *Renegat*. She could have found the captain, back when the ship had an actual captain. Or any of the officers, because the ship believed that the officers should always be available.

(Well, the ship didn't believe anything; the Fleet had set up all the ships that way.)

But finding lower level crew and non-crew? They had some kind of privacy protections that she couldn't easily overcome.

And this entire ship was now made up of lower-level crew.

Maybe she could find them by piggybacking off the system everyone used to track friends. She used to use it to track India, and, once upon a time, India used it to track her. Maybe India still used it to track her—which would explain how India always ended up near her.

Great. India. Misusing something designed to promote friendship and families. How very typical.

Serpell took a deep breath. She knew she was on edge, and when she was on edge, she made everything into a catastrophe—or so India used to say.

Like so many things that India said there was enough truth to the words to make Serpell nervous.

But this actually might be a catastrophe, especially if someone had been isolated behind that destruction from the shooting.

All of the crew had had training on what to do if they suddenly lost atmosphere. They were supposed to calmly (yeah, calmly. Right.) don an environmental suit, communicate with the bridge that there was a problem (if possible, of course), and wait for rescue.

Kabac—of all people—had reiterated that training shortly after the *Renegat* started its trip back from the Scrapheap.

Everyone needs to remember how to save themselves, he had said by way of explanation to Serpell, *because we sure as hell can't save them.*

But they could try.

And she didn't want someone to be waiting for a rescue that never came. Partially because she could imagine what that was like, and partially because at some point, she would learn about whoever died, and the guilt would cripple her.

She opened the system, leaned forward for an old-fashioned retinal scan, and the system automatically brought up the only person she had ever asked to track.

India.

Who was only six yards away.

Serpell took a step back from the control panel and looked down the ruined corridor. What was India doing down there? Was she the person trapped?

Serpell's heart suddenly started pounding so hard that it felt like it was going to hammer through her chest.

Had that damage come from the inside?

Had India sabotaged the ship?

And what was it about Serpell that made her think that her wife would try to damage the ship from the inside out?

Serpell clenched her fists, then contacted the bridge.

"Gajra," she said. "Did you ever find any life signs on Deck Four?"

"Besides yours?" Blaquer asked.

Time wasting. Serpell nearly said that, but being goaded into a fight would take even more time.

"Yes," she said, trying to keep her voice calm.

"I'm only seeing one other life sign," Blaquer said, which made it sound like she hadn't looked until right now. Proving Serpell's point about the total incompetence of the crew. "It's right near the door to the cargo bay. I can't tell if it's inside or outside."

"Identification?" Serpell asked, hoping against hope that the system she'd been using had gotten the identification wrong.

"Um," Blaquer said, sounding hesitant. "It looks like India Romano."

Serpell let out a breath. "Okay. Nothing else? No one else?"

"Not that I can see," Blaquer said. Serpell had never heard her sound so uncomfortable. Blaquer was usually confrontational, not uncertain. "But I can only read life signs…"

The way her voice trailed off made it clear what she was thinking. There might be some dead crew members inside that isolated area.

"Um, do me a favor," Serpell said. "Call up life signs all over the ship. Do a count. If you have 200, then we know we've accounted for everyone."

She hoped she didn't have to say what would happen if she didn't find 200. She liked to assume that her crew knew how to think for themselves, but she didn't trust it.

She didn't trust any of it.

"Okay," Blaquer said. "I'll let you know."

Serpell mouthed a curse. She wanted to know now. But she couldn't get Blaquer to move any quicker.

Instead, Serpell opened the environmental system again, and made certain that the environment down that corridor was safe for her. Otherwise, she'd have to get an environmental suit of her own before going, which would waste even more time.

The system told her that the environment was compromised but no suit was necessary.

Whatever that meant.

The very idea of that left her cold.

She shut down the systems, closed the panel door, and turned, facing the corridor, with its blinking lights, and residual smoke. If that was smoke. It might have been dust and debris from whatever damage had occurred down there.

Life sign.

Which meant India was alive.

But Serpell couldn't tell from the images she had looked at if India was inside or outside the damaged area.

Serpell stepped into the ruined corridor. Bits and pieces of ceiling and wall were scattered across the ground. Things she couldn't identify, things that looked like tubes and shards of blackness stuck out of areas on the walls, as if someone had punched them from the inside.

She assumed some kind of blast caused all this damage. Because if something else had—a person, say, or some ongoing damage, then she had no idea what she would do about it.

She picked her way cautiously over the debris. She could hear India's voice in her head, taunting her.

Why aren't you hurrying? Have you come to hate me that much?

Which wasn't true, but India would accuse her of it, and then Serpell would deny it, and India wouldn't believe her, and then they would fight, and—

Serpell's eyes pricked with tears. It was because of the ghostly smoke (or whatever that white stuff was) that hung in the corridor. She disturbed it when she walked, but it didn't dissipate which either meant the environmental system was compromised down here or it meant that something was still—burning? Changing? Causing the white stuff?

If only she had had some engineering training. Just a little. She would probably know what that white stuff was, whether or not it was bits of the corridor itself or smoke or something she had to worry about.

And, she realized as she stepped over a pile of shards and tubes, if the environmental system was malfunctioning, then that meant that it wouldn't be able to count the oxygen use and tell her how many people were here.

Her mouth was dry. It was amazing she could have seen India's life signs at all—even though that hadn't come through the environmental system. That reading was a different system. But still.

The deeper Serpell got into the corridor, the dimmer it became. Her throat burned, and she wished she had an environmental suit after all. The air tasted of metal, and her eyes were still watering.

Strings of nanobits (she thought) hung down from the ceiling, brushing against her hair, making her reflexively wipe at it, even though she couldn't make that feeling go away at all.

Then she reached the cargo bay. A white screen covered one wall, glimmering in the darkness. She extended a hand, her entire arm shaking. Then her fingers brushed the screen.

It was warm and solid, apparently holding back the vacuum of space.

"I'd stay away from that."

It took Serpell a few seconds to realize that India's voice was real, and not inside Serpell's head.

She turned toward the voice.

India was leaning against the opposite wall, arms crossed. She wore an environmental suit, but didn't have the hood up.

"Took you long enough," she said. "People could have died down here."

Serpell felt the words like a blow.

"Who's in there?" she asked.

India shrugged. "Why don't you check? Oh, that's right. You're not even prepared. An environmental suit would be advised."

"Is there one around here?" Serpell asked.

India half-smiled. Serpell used to love that expression. It was so wry. She used to find it amusing.

Now she wanted to slap it off India's face.

"You really don't know, do you?" India said. "You're so inept you don't even know where the environmental suits are stored."

India was right: she hadn't looked. Serpell hadn't thought all of this through.

"And you think you're qualified to be captain." India shook her head. "Your bridge. Your ship. As if you know anything about ships."

Serpell shook with fury. It would be so easy to jump into this fight. But she couldn't. Not right now.

There were more important tasks in front of her.

"Did you check to see if anyone was inside there?" Serpell asked. "Someone might be waiting to be rescued."

"Yeah, they might, and they might be dead by now." India pushed off the wall. "But you only thought of that now, and of course, you didn't send anyone to check for you, back when the people inside *could* have been rescued."

Oh, crap. There had been people in the area, and they had died. Because Serpell didn't know how to command a ship. Because she couldn't multi-task the way that so many Fleet officers could.

Because she couldn't get her crew (*her* crew) to listen to her.

"Did you get them out?" Serpell asked, her voice trembling.

"Did *I* get them out?" India took a step toward her. The movement actually felt threatening. "Me, the person who caused—what did you say?—twelve deaths. The person who doesn't think about anyone but herself? You expect that person to rescue crew members trapped in a damaged part of the ship, where the environmental system has failed and the gravity is gone and there's nothing holding them in place but their problem-solving skills and their ability to strap themselves into an area? That person?"

Serpell's face warmed. She glanced over her shoulder at that protective barrier. She didn't even know how to get in there, or if the system would let her in there.

"Yes, that person." Serpell's voice sounded weak and scratchy, partly from the chemical stench in the corridor, and partly because she was close to breaking apart. "You are wearing an environmental suit."

"Because anyone with brains wouldn't come down this corridor without wearing one," India snapped.

"But you're not wearing the hood," Serpell blurted before she could stop herself.

India's eyebrows went up in mock surprise. "You think that the greatest danger here is a lack of oxygen? There's oxygen. But all this other crap is harmful to us. I took off the hood when I heard you coming. Didn't think you'd recognize me with the hood on, and, I figured, you would scream and run if I approached out of this gray dusty stuff."

Serpell liked to believe she wouldn't run. She liked to believe she was stronger than that.

"We don't have time to fight," she said. "We have to get in there, and save people."

"Too late," India said. "That barrier is solid. Bet you didn't know that those things solidify up at a certain point, making rescues impossible. So you've just left crew members to die, slowly and hideously. How does it feel? You lost some of *your* crew, *Captain*."

Serpell started shaking. She tried not to let anyone die. She didn't want anyone to die. They shouldn't have died at all.

She had been so mad at India for getting people killed, but Serpell had done the same thing.

If she had only been down here sooner...

Then she glanced at India. India's half-smile had turned into a smirk. Had she been lying? Had she been simply trying to irritate Serpell, to unnerve her?

Serpell walked over to the barrier, and tried to see if there was a way inside. There had to be, right? There had to be a way to replace it, to fix the interior, so that—

"Leave it alone, Raina," India said. "You can't get in. The barrier will be there as long as the nanobits are repairing the hull."

The flush in Serpell's face grew warmer. How did India know that about nanobits? How did India know any of this?

Serpell moved around the barrier, trying to see past it. She couldn't. She leaned her head against the broken wall of the corridor. The wall felt warm against her skin. She let out a small sigh.

She couldn't have gotten here sooner. Everyone on the ship would have died if she had come down here sooner.

She had handled all of the different crises, all of them, and still people died.

And then she froze for just a second as an idea struck her.

She stood up and turned, the blood leaving her face, her heart pounding, but differently than it had before. The pounding felt like a fist pounding against the palm of the other hand, as if her heart itself was preparing for a fight.

"Why didn't you save them?" she asked.

India's eyes were hooded, almost impossible to see.

"You were here. You were waiting for me," Serpell said. "Why didn't you save them?"

"We already talked about this," India said.

"We didn't," Serpell said. "You deflected. You deflected because you didn't even try, did you? It would've been too much work for you to save them. You were waiting for someone else to get here, and then you were going to take all of the credit, weren't you? But no one came. *And you never called for help, did you?*"

"Are you accusing me of letting even more people die?" India asked.

"Yes," Serpell said.

India shook her head slightly. "I'll always be the bad guy to you, won't I?"

"You're not answering again," Serpell said. "Why didn't you go in and save everyone?"

"Stop trying to make this about me," India said.

The fury that Serpell had been repressing rose. "It *is* about you. You wanted to get at me. You twice repeated what I said on the bridge. I made you mad, and you just wanted to make me mad. You don't care about anyone else. You didn't save anyone because that's not who you are. You get people killed—"

"So do you," India said.

Serpell launched herself at India, grabbing her throat, and slamming her head against that wall. India looked so surprised that she didn't move for a moment.

Then Serpell slammed India's head again. Her head thudded against that wall, and cracks formed.

"You have done everything you can to make me feel worthless," Serpell said, "and now you're killing people to do it. You're killing them. You're pure evil, that's what you are. Pure evil."

India's hands grabbed at Serpell's wrists. India's fingernails cut into Serpell's skin, but she didn't care. India's fingers finally managed to grab on, but she couldn't pull away.

So she leaned backward, as if she was trying to brace herself.

Serpell pushed India into that wall, as hard as she could.

"You are the worst human being I have ever met," Serpell said. "You're selfish and self-involved and no one exists but you. You led twelve people to their deaths, and now all of these people. You killed them. You destroy everything you touch."

Serpell shoved India hard. The wall audibly cracked. India's head moved backward, and her eyes widened with alarm. She clawed at Serpell's hands, so Serpell yanked them away.

She was done shoving India. Serpell had made her point.

India reached up to her neck, then brought her arms down. Her hands hit the side of the wall, and it collapsed in on itself.

India fell backward, her body landing sideways, her head twisted to the right.

Black wall shards were cutting into the side of her neck, and blood was pouring into India's environmental suit. One of those tubes was stuck in her lower back.

India's eyes fluttered, and her mouth moved, but no sound came out.

"Oh, crap," Serpell said. She hadn't expected the wall to collapse. Walls on ships did not collapse. She had never heard of walls collapsing, not ever.

Serpell got on her knees and grabbed India's shoulders, trying to pull her away.

But the shards were stuck deeply in India's skin. Serpell couldn't just pull her back, and even if she did, she wouldn't be able to stop the bleeding.

She took one of India's hands and placed it on a bloody part of India's neck. "Hold that," Serpell said. She remembered that much of her emergency medical training. "Tight. I'll be right back."

And this time she sprinted down the destroyed corridor, back to the communications panel. She tripped three times, nearly fell once, caught her hand on a nearby wall (she thought) and felt a slice of pain through the palm. She'd been cut too.

Her breath was coming in ragged gasps, her chest aching, that metallic taste in her mouth so foul she was nearly gagging.

She staggered to the wider area around the elevators, her eyes gummy and her clothes splashed with blood. The air seemed clearer here, the lights brighter, but the stench of burned chemicals still covered everything.

She slapped her good hand on the control panel and it bounced open, but not before she noticed that she had left a bloody palm print on it. She hit the voice command, shouted, "Send a gurney. Send a gurney now!"

And then she contacted the med bay and told them to be on alert for a gurney, floating its way toward them. Serpell wasn't sure India would survive that. She wasn't sure anyone could.

Finally, she contacted the bridge. She wasn't sure who she got—one of the men, not Kabac. She would have recognized Kabac—and said, "India's hurt. And some people might be stuck in that area being repaired. Please, send help. Send help!"

The voice that answered her, deep, deceptively calm, said, "No one is stuck."

"Yes," she said. "Yes. India said that there were others. Please—"

"We did a head count, Raina." Patient. Calm. Kellman? Most likely. "Everyone is accounted for. No one is trapped, now that you got India out."

Got India out? Serpell didn't understand the reference. His words were barely registering.

No one was trapped? How could that be? India had said—

India. Had said. India.

"What do you mean out?" Serpell asked.

"The system showed us. She'd been inside that area," Kellman said. "Maybe checking to make sure everyone was all right."

That didn't fit. Something about what he said didn't fit. And India had known that the hull was breached. How had she known that? And why hadn't the repairs trapped her inside? They had started on the other spots before Serpell arrived down here. Why wouldn't the repairs start here at the same time? If they had, they would have trapped India. But she had time to put on an environmental suit…

A shiver ran through Serpell. She didn't have time to think about this. She would ask India later, and India would say, *You always make me the villain.* Then India would smile that horrid smile.

Serpell made herself focus, tried to set aside the fury that had returned a thousand fold.

"Okay," Serpell said. "Okay. Whatever. Just send someone. India's hurt and I have to get back to her."

And then she slammed the control panel door shut, accidentally using her injured hand. She cried out with pain, saw even more blood dripping onto the floor.

She ripped off part of her shirt, and used her good hand in combination with her teeth to wrap the rag around her palm. Then she scurried back down the corridor, a little slower than she had run out of it, because she didn't want to trip again. The top of her right foot was bruised from the last time, her left ankle ached, and her palm throbbed.

She hoped the gurney would find them in time. She needed help with India.

This time, Serpell knew where all the piles of debris were, and she slowed as she approached them, picking her way over them. She went as fast as she safely could, even though each minute felt like forever.

She didn't call out to India, not just because she had a hunch it would be hard for India to answer, but also because she didn't want to hear India's answer when it came.

It would be filled with blame and accusations and this time, they would all be right.

You hurt me. You left me here, bleeding. You left me. You. Left. Me.

Serpell had. For the first time ever, she had left India to fend for herself. India had taken advantage of her from the moment they met, hiding behind Serpell's competence, using Serpell as her scapegoat, getting Serpell blamed for India's mistakes.

And Serpell had stayed at her side through it all, taking the blame, defending India to others when they complained about the way that India treated them— and her. Coming onto this ship not because it was good for Serpell's career, but because it was India's last chance, ever.

Ever.

And then India had abandoned her when it became clear that Captain Preemas didn't respect anything Serpell did. India had emotionally dumped her for the captain, all the while pretending (to Serpell at least) that the marriage was fine. Just fine. Better than fine.

Even though Serpell had known that it wasn't.

Everyone had known.

The ache in her chest encompassed her heart as well as her lungs. The water dripping from her eyes almost felt like sloppy tears, and her nose was running. She swiped at it with the back of her good hand, stopping just before she reached India.

India couldn't see her like this, bloody with snot all over her face. India would think Serpell had gotten injured (she had, too, but she didn't want to tell India) and then India would accuse her of trying to get all of the attention.

India would tell Serpell that she was upstaging India who clearly had the more serious injuries, and she did. This time, India actually did.

Serpell stepped down that last part of the corridor. She saw India's legs first, the right one twisted outward, the left one bent in an acute angle that looked painful in and of itself.

The hand that Serpell had placed on India's neck, telling her to push hard, was laying across India's stomach, a blood streak running down the front of the environmental suit.

Dammit, India. She couldn't even follow that simple instruction. She needed to do that, or she would—

Die.

Serpell crouched.

India's eyes were open. The kelly green looked unnatural, like illuminated dials on an old-fashioned control board. India's mouth was open, slack and loose, like Serpell had never seen it, not even in sleep.

India's head was tilted sideways and where her neck should have been was a bloody meaty hole.

The collar of the environmental suit was thick with blood.

Serpell stared at it all in complete disbelief.

"India," she said softly. "This isn't funny. I get your point. Sit up."

But India didn't move. And even more weirdly, her eyes didn't close, her nostrils didn't flare like they sometimes did when she was trying to contain laughter. Her mouth remained open in that same weird way.

"India, don't mess with me," Serpell said. "Let's just call a truce, okay? You got a rise out of me. Two of them, really. Let's leave it at that."

Something banged in the corridor behind her, followed by a clang.

She looked up in time to see one of the automated gurneys, moving as if nothing was wrong, even though some of the nanobit strings clung to it like cobwebs on an abandoned part of a sector base.

Serpell was going to have to pick up India and place her on the gurney. The gurneys on the *Renegat* couldn't gather anyone like the gurneys on some of the DV-Class ships she had served on.

Serpell wasn't sure she could pick India up, not without injuring her worse. There were things sticking out of her, things attaching her to the wall.

The gurney bumped Serpell, as if nudging her to do the right thing.

It wouldn't help India to remain here. No matter what ripped as Serpell pulled her up, the rips could be repaired. She would bleed out here.

(She had bled out. She was dead. She was dead. She was dead.)

Serpell shook her head, blinking hard. Her eyes ached now, along with her throat, and her lungs and her heart. Maybe she was dying too, from the stench and the sheer terror she'd been under for weeks and weeks.

The gurney hit her one more time, with some force this time, and propelled her forward. She used the momentum to slip her arms under India's legs.

India didn't moan or even move. Serpell disconnected one of those tube things from India's back. India's environmental suit was tacky with drying blood.

Serpell bent her knees and braced one shoulder against what seemed like a secure part of the wall, then lifted. As she did, the gurney slipped underneath, and caught the lower half of India's body.

Then Serpell eased the upper half in place. Or tried to. Because India's head lolled back farther than a human head should have. Her head looked like it was going to fall off her neck. In the weird light, Serpell could see the tendons and the muscles and the blood vessels, which looked like popped balloons.

India would never allow something like that, not if she was conscious. And she wasn't conscious. She wasn't breathing.

She wasn't alive.

Serpell eased her onto the gurney, and then tapped it so that it would take India to the med bay. Then Serpell slid down the wall, holding her injured hand against her chest, her breath coming in great gasping sobs.

India couldn't be dead. Someone like India didn't die. Especially like that.

Serpell let out a shaky breath. She had shoved India, wrapped her hands around India's neck, had been so furious at India that she wanted India to die—

And maybe she had.

Because there had been no reason for India to be down here. No reason for her to be inside that cargo bay. No reason for her to know about the damage, the damage that was somehow worse than the other areas that had gotten hit during that last volley of shots.

And the tone of India's voice: *Your bridge. Your ship. As if you know anything about ships.*

India had deflected, not because she hadn't tried to rescue people, but because she had made the damage worse. Then she was going to try to clean up the mess, to prove to the entire ship that Serpell wasn't qualified to be captain. That *India* should be in charge.

Serpell closed her eyes for a brief moment. She was trying to justify her own actions, make herself feel better about what she had done.

But she didn't feel better. It would have been better to have the fight with India, to prove to the entire ship that India was self-centered and crazy and dangerous.

If Serpell told anyone what happened, they would think that she had killed India on purpose. And she hadn't. She hadn't done anything on purpose. None of her actions, from the moment the ship had reached the Scrapheap, had been on purpose. She had had nothing to do with the captain's death, and what happened to the engineers—well, they left the ship voluntarily. They were no longer her problem.

And now India.

She ran a filthy hand over her face, wincing at the stickiness of the blood. She felt an odd mixture of relief and sheer terror. The terror was easier to unpack. She hadn't lived without India for more than a decade. Serpell wasn't even sure how to be without India. Serpell wasn't even sure who she was any more.

Although others seemed to see her clearly. Others respected her. Others knew that India was the screw-up, not Serpell.

Others respected Serpell. Maybe it was time that she learned to respect herself.

That thought jolted the rest of the terror, made it even worse. Because she had just screwed up. She hadn't known walls could shatter like that, but maybe the others did. Maybe they would tell her she should have thought of that.

And maybe she should have.

But it was an accident. No one could plan for accidents.

Serpell swallowed hard. She looked up. The clouds of whitish stuff still wafted by. And the environmental system only partially worked. The corridors were monitored, but if the environmental system was down, then maybe the rest of the system was down.

She made herself stand up, and it felt like she hadn't stood for days and days and days. She wobbled, then caught the wall with her bad hand, wincing with the pain.

But the pain was good for her. It clarified her thoughts.

If there had been visual imagery available when Serpell had started her search for survivors, the system would have shown her the imagery. But she had to make certain.

Because…what had Kellman said? He had said *No one is trapped, now that you got India out.*

India had lied about that. Serpell shuddered again, the fury temporarily back, and she tamped it down, something she always did—had done since she met India. She had tamped down her feelings.

Which was why they had come roaring out.

Serpell's hand shook as she examined the visual footage. The equipment told her that it was malfunctioning; the cameras went out after the first shots hit this part of the *Renegat.*

There were no images of the corridor, which meant no images of her shoving India, of the wall breaking, which meant no images of anything. Not a bit of it.

Serpell made herself focus, punching in even more commands. She tried (again) to see if she could see what was behind that barrier, and there were no visuals from that either. The visuals there were completely gone.

But she did find something else. The initial damage behind that barrier hadn't been bad. The damage had gotten worse, only in one spot. She tried to focus on that spot, and couldn't.

But India had been inside. And the damage had gotten worse.

Serpell closed her eyes. She could take care of all of the messaging around this. There was no way anyone could know what had happened in that corridor without Serpell saying.

… now that you got India out…

The entire crew had thought India was trapped behind that barrier, and that Serpell had saved her.

Serpell straightened.

She would say she had gotten there at the last minute. She wouldn't tell them why India had been inside that barrier. Let them believe what they wanted.

Only Serpell would tell them that when she arrived, India was already dying. Serpell had gotten her out, but had to go for help, and in the meantime, India had died, all alone on that corridor floor.

She would confess to finding India, nothing more. And that was the thing: no one would question her. They would all believe that India had done something stupid, because how many times in the past had India done something stupid.

Most of the time, really. And they all knew it, and secretly felt sorry for Serpell.

But not anymore.

Her relief was making her lightheaded, or maybe it was the blood loss. The cloth bandage she had tied around her palm was black and saturated.

She pressed the call button for another gurney, this one for her, then she sank onto the floor and put her head between her knees, holding on tight. The light-headedness wasn't fading. It was still there, maybe getting worse.

If Serpell went to the med bay with an injury, sustained here—one she hadn't had when she rescued the ship (and dammit, she *had* rescued the *Renegat*, something India never ever ever would have given her credit for)—and everyone would think she had sustained the injury trying to get her wife out of that dangerous area.

The key to everything was judicious silence. About India. About the mutiny. About the captain. About the engineers. If anyone asked about anything—anyone who had not been on the *Renegat*—all Serpell had to do was imply. The less she said, the better.

Starting now.

The gurney arrived, floating in the middle of that whitish debris. It lowered itself to her side, then bumped her like the other one had done.

This time, she couldn't really stand.

This time, she levered herself onto the gurney, then collapsed on her stomach, too weak to move.

She had underestimated her own strength. Or maybe she was injured worse than she had realized.

Or maybe it was just the emotion, the stress.

"Med bay," she said aloud to the gurney, not sure if she had to give it instructions. But she did.

And it floated her out of this corridor, away from the site of her crime, away from the reality of what had happened, what India had done to the ship, and what Serpell had done to India.

Serpell closed her eyes and let herself drift.

She was going to survive this. Not just the loss of India or the damage India had inflicted.

Serpell was going to make this crew—her crew—work together.

On her bridge. On her ship.

They would follow her lead.

And she was going to get them all home.

No matter what it took.

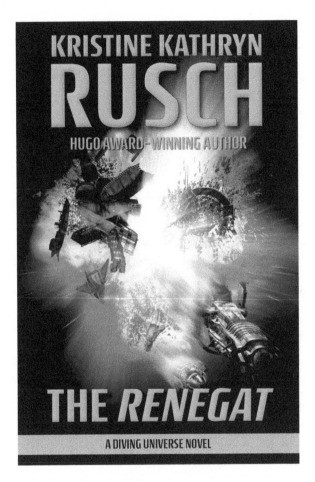

KRISTINE KATHRYN
RUSCH

HUGO AWARD-WINNING AUTHOR

THE *RENEGAT*

A DIVING UNIVERSE NOVEL

The adventure continues in Kristine
Kathryn Rusch's award-winning Diving
Universe with *The Renegat*, on sale now.
Turn the page for a sample.

THE SCRAPHEAP

INTERNAL CLOCK MALFUNCTION
PERPETUAL NOW

THE SCRAPHEAP

THE FORCE FIELD BREACH CAUGHT THE SCRAPHEAP'S attention. It tried to enter the breach properly into its log, but could not cite a date. The Scrapheap did not have the capacity to manufacture a date, so its systems awoke.

It needed assistance. Human assistance.

The Scrapheap did not know how long it had functioned without human assistance. Its internal clock had doubled over on itself three times and had malfunctioned on the fourth reset. That malfunction did not trigger an alarm, because it was no threat to the Scrapheap itself.

The Scrapheap monitored and evaluated threats. Its protocols demanded that it record major breaches and threats from outside. Internal threats were dealt with routinely.

Energy spikes were minimized. Certain ships were contained within their own private force fields.

The Scrapheap had done such things since its beginning.

It did not think of its beginning as anything but the start of its internal clock. It was not self-aware, although certain systems had more awareness than other systems.

The Scrapheap knew its own history. It had started as five decommissioned ships, stored side by side in a region of space its creators believed to be little used and off the main travel routes for the sector. Those decommissioned ships were to be transferred to the nearest sector base, but the base had no need for the ships.

So the first force field was created. It protected all five ships. Those ships remained in the force field, and then other ships were added. Some were brought in under their own power. Others were towed in by a larger ship. Still others arrived using their *anacapa* drives.

On one occasion, those arrivals had caused a chain reaction. The energy wave from the arriving *anacapa* drive had triggered a malfunction in a dying *anacapa* drive, causing one ship to explode and resulting in damage to two more.

Humans had arrived three months later with a new core for the Scrapheap, and a control center to protect that new core. The Scrapheap's mission grew that day, to preserve and protect the ships and the ship parts inside its force field.

The Scrapheap followed its mission diligently, recording its activity, logging it, using the dates from its internal clock.

Over centuries, the Scrapheap grew from five ships to one million, three hundred and sixty-three thousand, seven hundred and one. Not all of the ships were intact. Many of the items the Scrapheap called ships were not ships at all, but parts of ships.

In the early centuries, the humans returned regularly, flashing their identifications and removing ships that still had value. The humans moved intact ships inside a secondary force field near the core, and did not touch those ships, although those ships routinely maintained themselves. If one of those ships malfunctioned, it would flag itself for removal from the secondary force field. If possible, the ship would then remove itself from the secondary force field.

If the ship could not move itself, the Scrapheap would do so, using a powerful tractor beam that only existed inside the secondary force field.

The Scrapheap maintained all of the external shields that belonged to the ships gathered in the main force field. In that way, those ships would not spark another disaster. The Scrapheap added and removed miniature force fields, rotated some ships away from others, kept those with dying *anacapa* drives isolated from ships that could possibly negatively interact with the dying drives.

The humans went in and out of the Scrapheap, removing ships and parts of ships as needed. Some ships' *anacapa* drives were activated remotely, and those ships left the Scrapheap on their own power. Sometimes humans entered the Scrapheap through various portals built into the large exterior force field, and removed ships.

One thousand years into the Scrapheap's existence, the humans ceased removing ships. The only changes inside the Scrapheap were the ones the Scrapheap initiated itself.

Until the breach.

A ship tried to enter the Scrapheap. That ship did not know the code to activate the portal in the force field, so the Scrapheap activated its defenses.

The ship left.

This was not unusual. It happened routinely throughout the Scrapheap's existence, so the Scrapheap did not create a log for the incident, although the incident remained in the short-term buffers.

Then the ship returned. It used a code that had not been used since the first four hundred years of the Scrapheap's existence.

The force field opened.

The ship entered the Scrapheap, flew around many of the ships inside the Scrapheap, and left.

The ship repeated this behavior for two hours on each of the next five days.

On the sixth day, the ship returned. It followed a path it had used before, and stopped near a DV-Class ship. Humans then emerged from the returning ship, and traveled to the DV-Class ship. The humans entered the DV-Class ship, and one-point-two hours later, the *anacapa* drive inside that ship activated.

The DV-Class ship left the Scrapheap.

The new ship remained inside the Scrapheap. The Scrapheap tried to contact that new ship. It did not respond. The new ship eventually left via engine power through the opening in the force field.

The Scrapheap then tried to identify the type of ship that the new ship had been. That type of ship did not exist in the Scrapheap's records. Nor did the ship seem to be a ship that could have been updated from any other ship in the Scrapheap's records.

The Scrapheap had scenarios programmed into its systems for such an occurrence. The scenarios postulated that the ship had stolen the entry codes and was now stealing vessels.

The Scrapheap would attack the ship when it returned. But it did not return.

Instead, the DV-Class vessel returned. Humans, identified as the same or similar to the ones who had arrived earlier, traveled from the returning DV-Class vessel to another DV-Class vessel. Then the second DV-Class vessel's *anacapa* drive activated, and removed the second DV-Class vessel from the Scrapheap. Then the first DV-Class vessel left again.

At that moment, the Scrapheap attempted to log the interaction as a serious breach. It could not do so. It no longer had the ability to time-stamp a log.

The Scrapheap had a failsafe to send information to its creators should the log function break down. But that failsafe had limitations.

The Scrapheap had to send the information from its short-term buffers to the humans before the information was recycled out of the buffers.

Upon discovering that it needed to send the information from the short-term buffers, the Scrapheap acted immediately. It sent the information along the channels it had been using for its decennial updates.

The Scrapheap also requested a repair of its systems as well as an augmentation that would prevent the unwarranted theft of vessels.

It could not attack vessels that had been stored inside the Scrapheap.

But it could flag the breaches as suspicious, maintain the records of those breaches, until the human creators arrived and determined what to do with the information.

Because the buffered information needed to be protected differently than the decennial update and because the buffered information could not be permanently stored, the Scrapheap requested a receipt be sent when the information reached its final destination.

The Scrapheap had not made such a request in all of its existence. The request set different protocols into place, protocols the Scrapheap had never used before.

The information system was old. The buffered information first traveled to sector bases closed, abandoned, and forgotten. The information then routed back to the Scrapheap, which repackaged the information and sent the information again.

The Scrapheap repackaged six times before the information managed to get through that hurdle in the system.

The Scrapheap then deleted the previous sector bases from its communications channel. It sent information directly to the working sector base.

More ships disappeared weekly, so the Scrapheap sent buffered information weekly.

The Scrapheap did not get a response.

Its systems were programmed to continue to send information until it received instructions.

It received none.

So it continued to send, even as the buffer cleaned itself out, and the log mechanism jammed. The Scrapheap did close the force field and reactivate the defensive measures, but sanctioned DV-Class vessels continued to enter the Scrapheap, disgorge humans to another DV-Class vessel, and then remove that DV-Class vessel.

The emptiness inside the Scrapheap grew.

The Scrapheap was not alarmed by this change. The Scrapheap was not sentient.

But it responded like any powerless being under attack.

It asked for help.

It defended itself as best it could, while it waited for a response.

PART ONE
THE JOYRIDE
130 YEARS AGO

THE *BRAZZA TWO*

THEY ASSEMBLED IN THE THIRD LEVEL MESS HALL, the one designed for first-years. The furniture was tiny, built for small bodies, and the walls had painted murals of cats and dogs, the comfort animals kept in the arboretum wing, and not allowed on this level. Still, Nadim Crowe knew, a lot of tears got shed beneath those murals, hiccoughy tears, the kind that little kids couldn't hold back even if they wanted to.

He thought the murals cruel, but then, he thought sending little kids to boarding school while their parents gallivanted across the universe equally cruel. Last year, he'd volunteered down here until the sobs got to him. Then he requested a transfer, which had sent him to the medical wing, and that turned out to be infinitely worse.

Why he'd decided on the Third Level Mess as a meeting site for the two teams was beyond him. It went into that category of his existence that he filed under *It Seemed Like A Good Idea At The Time.*

Of course, he hadn't thought that through until tonight, while he was waiting for the others to arrive. Before that, he'd only thought about the competition. He had had a lot of prep to do, and that meant doing some of the prep here, in the Third Level Mess.

A week ago, he'd tampered with the Third Level Mess's security system, shutting down the audio and video tracking just to see if anyone noticed the system had been tampered with. He kept the environmental controls on and boosted the emergency warnings, just in case something bad happened here while the security system was off. The Mess was all about little kids, after all.

He had chosen the middle of Ship Night, when (in theory) no little kids were using the Mess. He'd kept the system down for three hours just to see if anyone noticed.

No one did notice, which disturbed him and relieved him in equal measures. He didn't like that it was so easy to tamper with the security systems on the *Brazza Two*, but at the same time, it made this little dare easier.

And, he knew, that the systems in other parts of the ship, systems that monitored kids his age, were better designed. The adults didn't think that little-little kids would meddle with security systems, but the adults knew that teens did. Crowe supposed if any of the little-littles had successfully screwed with a security system, they would have moved to the gifted track immediately.

He had no idea how the gifted track worked for the littlest of kids. He hadn't been on this ship when he was really little. He had arrived on the ship at age nine. Unlike most kids, he'd actually requested his berth. He'd already been old enough to know that anywhere in the universe was better than a landlocked life with his parents, so why not go to the best possible school which had the added bonus of being in space as well.

The fading bruises, two broken ribs, and evidence of other badly healed broken bones had convinced the Fleet's school administrators that Crowe had been right about his parents. His tests—off the charts when it came to mathematics, science, and technical aptitude—convinced the administrators to send him to the most prestigious school ship in the Fleet.

He never would have cried underneath these murals if he had arrived here when he was young enough to eat in the Third Level Mess. He would have celebrated.

He wasn't celebrating now. He was jittery.

He'd been the first to arrive in the Third Level Mess, and it was mostly dark. Five dim overhead lights failed to properly illuminate the space. Four of the lights were in the Mess's four corners, leaving pools of darkness over the tables and the back area.

The fifth light—the brightest light—was off to his right. It shone over the long rectangular counter designed for the adult staff to serve the little kids their food. When he volunteered here, he wondered why there was a serving station. After all, in the other messes, the students were monitored by computer and actually informed when they took a food item that didn't fit into their regulation diet.

He asked his question, and was told that computer diet controls caused most of the little-littles to melt down. Instead, it was better to have adult assistance, so when a child did break down, he did so with someone nearby who could soothe him.

Crowe had seen a lot of soothing here, more than he had experienced at home. He'd also seen a lot of unhappy children. Because of that, he knew, most people on the *Brazza Two* avoided the Third Level Mess.

No one monitored this section of the ship after dinner either. He had double- and triple-checked that himself when he had come here in preparation for the competition. He had gotten the idea, and before he had even told Tessa about it, he had gone to the three main competition sites—the Mess and two different ship bays—to see if the competition was even possible.

It was—just barely. It would take some luck and a whole bunch of skill. That was what he loved about it, and that was why he was so very excited.

In the last fifteen minutes, his team had started to arrive. Ten of his friends, sliding in one at a time, some of them fist-bumping him as they passed, others just hovering near the bench beneath the mural, which provided the only truly comfortable seating. The bench was at adult height, probably because whoever built it had had some kind of brain fart, and had forgotten that this room was for little-littles.

As the team arrived, Crowe stood with his hands behind his back, deliberately mimicking Captain Mbue's favorite posture. She impressed him. She had been the captain since he started here. She was no-nonsense. When she gave her annual do-your-best speech to the various classes, she meant it. Some of the other teachers and staff on the ship treated the students with barely concealed condescension, but Captain Mbue seemed to believe each word she said.

When Crowe became captain—a real captain, a captain of a DV-Class vessel—he would treat his entire crew with respect, from the oldest to the youngest. He would do his best to be exactly like Captain Mbue.

And tonight, he was going to captain a ship. If he pulled this off, no one on the *Brazza Two* would be the wiser. Or if they found out, they would think him brazen but brilliant. He hoped for the first, but he would take the second.

The question was whether or not he would still run the mission if Tessa failed to show up.

Tessa Linley, the most gorgeous girl he had ever seen. She was luminescent, with dark brown eyes that perfectly matched her smooth unblemished skin. She wore her long hair in dozens of tiny braids that fell down her back most of the time, but when she was working hard on something delicate, she would wrap those braids around the top of her head like a crown.

He had no idea if she knew that half of the competitions and challenges he had thrown at her had been because he wanted to see her marvelous brain at work and because he wanted to spend more time with her. He had yet to impress her, although he had won two of the past three challenges he had made to her.

None had been as elaborate as this one. They had come up with it together. They had found some redundant systems in the *Brazza Two's* security protocols. Thinking they had happened on something the more experienced engineers had missed, Tessa and Crowe had asked one of their instructors if they could begin the process of removing the redundant systems.

The instructor had laughed, which surprised both of them. And then he had complimented them on their observations.

But, he had said, *those systems exist for a reason. This is a school ship with the best and brightest in the Fleet on board. We've learned over the years that no matter how hard we try to keep you students intellectually stimulated, you'll still venture out on your own. And one of the things you'll do is tamper with the systems. The redundancies make sure that the tampering and the damage from it are at a minimum.*

Crowe and Tessa said nothing to each other for days after that, but slowly they realized that they both had come to the same conclusion: they both decided to investigate the redundancies, to see what the "best and brightest" had tried before Crowe and Tessa had even thought of boarding the *Brazza Two.*

That, combined with the fact that the *Brazza Two* had followed a part of the Fleet to a nearby Scrapheap for some major learning opportunity for the officer candidates, had captured Crowe's imagination. Not only did he want to best the students who had come before him in the accelerated youth program, he also wanted to visit that Scrapheap, and he knew he wouldn't be allowed to.

Only the officer candidates—those in their twenties or older, with decades of schooling and experience beneath them—were allowed to go. And they would be supervised every moment of the visit, which sounded like torture to Crowe.

He loved working on his own. And that, combined with the other strictures, had given him an idea.

Tessa then refined it.

And like almost everything they came up with, they decided to turn it into a competition.

Unlike their other competitions, though, this one required the help of others. Together, Tessa and Crowe recruited half of their class.

Tessa sidled up beside him. He knew she was there before he saw her. The scent of her jasmine soap always preceded her. She leaned against him, her soft skin warm against his, and he felt a jolt of lust.

He took one step away. He didn't want to be distracted by his body right now.

"Wasn't sure you were going to come," he said softly.

"And miss this? Are you kidding?" She stepped forward just a bit, probably so that she could see his face in the dim light.

He could see hers, bright and eager and shining with excitement.

"You do a head count?" she asked.

"Not yet," he said. "I was waiting for you."

She punched his arm lightly. "We don't have a lot of time. You should've been ahead of this."

"You're the one who's late," he said.

"I'm not late," she said. "You were early."

"Still want to do this?" he asked, deflecting. Or maybe just deflecting the thoughts from his brain.

Maybe that was why he didn't win every contest he had with Tessa. Part of his brain was always busy controlling his body so that she wouldn't know just how much she affected him. Another part of his brain monitored his every word so that he wouldn't say something stupid. That part of his brain usually failed, especially as he got deeper into the contest and focused on the task at hand instead of his mouth.

Fortunately, Tessa didn't insult easily.

She didn't forget, though, either, and she often brought those comments back up, usually in a teasing way, but still. He found his missteps horribly embarrassing.

"If I didn't want to do this," she said, "I wouldn't be here. What I'm not sure about is whether or not we can finish before everyone gets up. I don't want to come back to a welcoming committee."

He bit his lower lip. They had discussed this problem earlier, and then she had said it didn't bother her.

"It's a possibility," he said. "A good one. That's why I'm asking you if you want to back out."

She let out a half laugh, and her eyes sparkled. She was so beautiful when she was smiling that it took his breath away.

"Are you kidding?" she asked. "It's been ages since we've done anything remotely exciting. I've been looking forward to this for weeks."

"So have I," he said, feeling a spike of energy running through him. "So let's get to it."

She nodded, then started a head count, whispering the numbers under her breath. He counted with her, mentally making note of which team the people present were on.

His team had gathered together near the mural wall. Hers was scattered around the room, huddling together in twos and threes. That one simple fact buoyed him. It meant his team was more cohesive than hers.

"Looks like everyone's here," she said.

Not only were both teams in place, but each member was the correct member. Once, he'd initiated a competition with Tessa, and half the people he'd handpicked to participate had sent someone else in their place. It had been a last-minute competition, though, and he really hadn't prepped anyone.

This time, he'd been running virtual drills with his team. He'd designed a three-part program that simulated what he thought would happen. The first part got the team to the docking bay. The second part was stolen from the flight simulator that first-year pilot training instructors used, and the third part was sheer guesswork.

Tessa had warned him not to do anything like that—*you'll get caught and then what will you say?* she asked; *I'll say that I was using my imagination just like they encourage,* he replied. But he hadn't gotten caught. And not only had he maintained the interest of his team in the adventure, he had also made sure they were as prepared as they could be.

"Okay." Tessa clapped her hands together to get everyone's attention. It was ten-thirty p.m. ship time. They weren't even supposed to start until eleven.

But Crowe had no problem with starting early. The earlier they left, the sooner they would return. If they managed to get back before four a.m., they were less likely to be caught.

Tessa had probably impressed that on her team; he certainly had on his.

"This is your last chance if you want to back out," Tessa was saying—to everyone, which kinda annoyed him. He didn't want anyone to back out and he didn't want to remind them that backing out was an option.

Everyone was watching her. He could see faces half-illuminated in the dim light, all of them focused on her with great intensity, which also irritated him. She was his friend, not theirs—although that wasn't true. Tessa somehow managed to be everyone's friend, even though she was closest to him—or so he hoped.

"There's a chance we could get caught," she said. "A good chance, really. But as I told you, or rather, as I told my team, there's safety in numbers. They might punish all of us, but not as severely as they'd punish one of us. So you'd be helping out in more ways than one if you stay. Besides, this'll be fun!"

Her voice rose with that last bit, and it actually sounded like fun instead of something scary and dangerous.

A bunch of people closest to Crowe smiled. He couldn't see the other faces clearly enough to know if they were smiling too.

He needed to take this over, though, before she scared them all to death.

He said, "Those of you who've been in competitions before with me and Tessa know the drill. We're going to have the computer start a thirty-second countdown. As soon as it hits zero, it'll say *Go!* and you go. You know where you're supposed to be, so you run there."

Or, he thought, his team knew where they were supposed to be. He had no idea if hers knew.

"You should have instructions from me or Tessa, so you should know what to do." He didn't look at her in case she failed at this for the first time ever. She used to be the most organized one of the two of them. She wasn't anymore—he had learned that lesson soundly and had started to beat her at her own game.

"If you don't know exactly," Tessa said, lending credence to the idea that she hadn't prepared as much as he had, "follow the other members of your team. My team is wearing a slash of lime green along one cheek tonight, so if you see someone with a slash across their face and you're part of my team, follow that person. Someone will put you to work."

He hadn't thought about color-coding his team, but that was only necessary for this part of the competition anyway. He had hardly given the front part of this any thought at all, because that wasn't the part that interested him.

The competition really didn't start until the teams got on board their respective ships.

"Remember," Tessa said, "the point of this is to have fun, and maybe learn something along the way."

Crowe disagreed: he thought the point was to learn something and maybe have fun along the way, but he stayed quiet. Tessa was better at rousing the troops than he was.

"So, ready?" Tessa asked. "The countdown starts…*now!*"

Apparently that was her computer command, because the androgynous voice started counting backwards from thirty.

Crowe moved slightly away from the door. He had instructed his team to let Tessa's go first. A few competitions ago, some of the team members had gotten trampled in the opening stampede, and that had cost him precious time (not to mention a long and convoluted explanation in the medical wing).

Besides, he hadn't just tampered with the security systems here; he'd also tampered with the door commands on the docking bay entrance his team was going to use.

The tampering wasn't as extreme as the tampering here—ship security would definitely have noticed any major changes to the systems in the docking bay.

All he had done was prep the redundant systems to operate more efficiently if given certain commands. He had figured, if he had gotten caught, that he would tell his teachers or security that he had been trying to improve the system. He'd been given permission to investigate the redundant systems after all.

The computer countdown hit *three...two...one...Go!* and Tessa's team took off so fast that they nearly trampled each other.

"See ya, sucker!" Tessa said to him as she raced by. He just smiled. She should have seen that as a warning that he had done some prep, but she hadn't.

Or maybe she just didn't care.

She was on her way to the secondary docking bay. It was closer to the Third Level Mess than the docking bay he had chosen. She probably thought the proximity would give her team an advantage.

But there was a lot that could eat up that advantage, including getting in, working the ship, and getting the bay doors to open. His team had worked through all of the scenarios he could think of, and he still worried that those hadn't been enough.

The sound of her team's shoes, slapping against the floor, receded. There was no laughing and giggling and catcalls, like there had been on some previous competitions, so she had done some work with her team.

"Okay," he said when he could no longer hear Tessa's team. "Let's go."

His team gathered around him, and they walked to the docking bay. No running at all. They even took the Third Level elevator to the First Level. Nothing wrong with students touring the public area of the ship. He'd learned that long ago. And if they weren't acting like they were doing something wrong, then no one would think they were.

Two of his team members—Omar and Erika—already had their personal computer screens up on clear holographic mode. They were the ones assigned with tricking the redundant systems so that the team could get into the docking bay undetected—at least for a few minutes. Long enough that they would be able to get to the ship he had chosen.

Two other team members—Igasho and Sera—were going to scrub the identities of the entire team, effectively removing them from the security system the moment the group entered the docking bay. He'd learned that trick by studying what students had done before.

The system was set up to catch that little maneuver, but he'd tested it (like he had tested everything), not with his own profile, but with the profiles of some of the kids one year ahead of him. He'd set up the scrubbing to look like it was accidental—a glitch in the system. And he'd deliberately chosen candidates who had no real technical expertise. These were the kids who liked the arts, who focused on languages or ship culture or Fleet history, such as it was.

There was no way those kids had the ability to scrub their own profiles, and they didn't have the wherewithal to hire someone (or bribe someone) to do it for them. If ship security didn't look too deeply at the scrubbing, no one would figure out what had happened.

So far, no one had looked to see if the scrubbing was anything more than a system error.

And Crowe had learned how long it took the system to recognize it had been spoofed and to solve the problem.

The fastest the scrubbing had been repaired had been seven minutes. The fastest it had been reported to a human had been ten minutes—and that had been on the same student. It had been an outlier, but Crowe used that figure as his figure.

He'd tested the team in their simulation. They had to move fast to the ship, and get inside within six minutes. That way, when their profiles returned to the system, they wouldn't be in the middle of boarding a ship they had no right to be on.

They hadn't done it physically—they hadn't done any of this physically—but they knew what the stakes were, and at least according to some of his instructors, virtual drills created brain muscle memory as effectively as actual drills created actual muscle memory.

He was counting on that.

The elevator door opened on First Level, and the team headed en masse to the docking bay entrance. Once inside, they'd run to the ship. Out here, they laughed and joked like kids on a walk, except for Omar and Erika, who were in the middle of the circle, mostly protected from the security imagery—so that the system wouldn't flag their behavior (or anyone's behavior) as suspicious.

The corridor was wide enough to accommodate four across, the ceilings high, and the floor made of a material he always meant to look up, designed to help anyone who had not yet adjusted to the peculiarities of the *Brazza Two* to maintain balance and stability. This flooring vanished on the main levels, but was part of the entire area around the docking bay, something Crowe had noticed, but didn't yet understand.

They arrived at the fifth entrance into this docking bay. This particular entrance had the most minimal security because it was the farthest from any access point. It also led into the part of the docking bay reserved for the lesser-used ships. No outside ships ever docked here, and no small ship in active use docked here either.

Crowe had spent nearly a week looking up each small ship in this area, its specs, its foibles, and its capacity. He knew he had an inexperienced team, so he wanted something easy to pilot. He also knew that the ship had to be large enough to handle ten, and with portholes big enough that the team could see the Scrapheap with their own eyes.

He also wanted a ship that could handle the distance to the Scrapheap rapidly, with minimum fuss, and could handle the one maneuver he was most afraid of on its own.

Bringing the ship back to the *Brazza Two* and docking in the same spot required piloting skills beyond anyone in this group. While all of the small ships attached to the *Brazza Two* had an autopilot function, not all of the autopilots worked well.

Most of that was by design. The *Brazza Two* didn't just train gifted students in their early years of study and scholars who would eventually train aboard a specialty ship; it also trained pilots, engineers, and the entire officer corps. They all needed small ship experience, and not all of that experience could come from simulations.

Many of the small ships in this docking bay were training vessels with certain features disabled or removed. Crowe needed all of the features of a Fleet vessel to work well, just in case his little crew did get into trouble. He needed to be able to activate a part of the ship or give it over to the computer or contact someone on the *Brazza Two*, ask for help, and then be able to implement that help.

He hoped nothing would go that seriously wrong on this little adventure, but he also knew that hope wasn't something a commander could count on.

Captain Mbue had said that on more than one occasion. Speaking to his class, she had added, *Hope should give us the wings to pursue the experience that will then enable us to make the best decisions for that particular moment. Optimism and hope built the Fleet. Experience pilots it. Adventure keeps it moving, ever forward.*

She had never mentioned creativity in any of her speeches, but Crowe liked to think that creativity was part of the Fleet as well. Maybe one of the most valuable parts.

Certainly, his creativity had helped him catch the attention of every single one of his teachers. They always gave him assignments far beyond anything someone his age should do. And they praised his nonstandard way of approaching each problem they gave him, telling him they had never met anyone who thought like he did.

He hoped they would have the same reaction to this adventure. If they caught him.

The fifth entrance into the docking bay was also the smallest—a single door. The eleven crowded around it, and waited while Adil took point. He was slender and small, having not yet hit his full growth, which Crowe believed might make him even more valuable down the road.

Right now, Adil had to unlock the entrance. Crowe was suddenly breathing shallowly. He wanted to unlock the entrance. He had done every single thing in the simulation, so he knew what the crew would be up against, and some things he did better than others.

Like opening doors undetected.

Only his time had been fifteen seconds *slower* than Adil's time. And nothing Crowe could do in the simulation made his time faster than Adil's.

That was how Crowe had made the assignments anyway. The crew members who did the jobs the swiftest while being the most accurate were the ones who got the job.

That didn't stop him from shifting from foot to foot. Each passing second felt like an hour.

He hadn't thought about this, about the way it looked when eleven kids crowded around a door. If he had given that part thought, he would have had the scrubbing of their digital signatures begin sooner.

Adil finished in record time (even though it didn't feel that way) and the door slid to one side, just like it was supposed to. The crew walked in, with Igasho and Sera remaining just outside the door, as they finished the scrubbing.

Or, at least, Crowe hoped they finished the scrubbing. Because this was one part of the plan that they had no way to check.

Igasho entered first. His black eyes met Crowe's, and Igasho nodded. Igasho believed it was done.

Then Sera stepped inside and shouted, "*Go!*" just like she was supposed to do.

The crew ran for the first time, everyone heading for the scout ship that Crowe had designated as theirs.

His stomach tightened, and he was still having trouble breathing. He'd checked and double-checked the manifest all day, just to make sure that the scout ship was still in place.

The ship had the uninspired name of *Br2 Scout3*. Apparently school ships lost scouts in training so often that the scouts' names were simple.

This scout had been in service for almost a hundred years, and was on its last legs. It hadn't been used much at all, which was one reason why Crowe had targeted it. He knew no one was paying much attention to it.

He'd run a diagnostic a few weeks ago, piggyback-ing on engineering's standard small ship diagnostic. So technically, *he* hadn't run the diagnostic at all. He had just added *Br2 Scout3* to the list, and the engineering depart-ment had run its usual check. The ship came out clean.

Crowe scurried around some of the other smaller ships—a runabout, an orbiter, a few tiny ships that were little more than pods—following his team.

He was the one in charge of the scout ship, and he had to get there when everyone else did, but he had a stitch in his side from his uneven breathing.

He was a lot more nervous than he expected to be. This entire mission was a lot more real than he had ever imagined, and he was beginning to think they were in too deep.

If he hadn't made this into a contest with Tessa, he might have backed out right here.

But he had, and his pride was going to keep him moving forward.

The team arrived at the ship with two minutes to spare. They were all gathered around the back end of the scout. This ship had a cargo door, like many of the mili-tary vessels.

Usually small ships were coded to the pilots and bridge crew of the larger vessel they rode in, but not training ships. Training ships had entry codes for each class that was supposed to train inside.

Crowe had investigated which unit was using what type of training ship at the moment. None of them were actually training on scout ships in classes right now, but the classes on the scout ships would start up in a few weeks.

Fortunately for him, the instructors for that unit were already preparing—or maybe they had never changed the entry codes. He had dug into that part of the shipboard computer, using an instructor identification he had borrowed long ago. It wasn't the only instructor identification he had borrowed in his time here—he rotated through them when he needed to.

He'd actually burned three of them on this trip. If the team got caught, he wouldn't be able to use those identifications again.

His mouth was dry and his heart was pounding. He stepped up to the back control panel, hidden to the left of the door. Usually this part of a scout ship was opened in the ship's tiny bridge, but there were redundant systems in all of the Fleet's vessels.

Every type of ship had extra ways to enter. Ships that went off on their own without any backup, like scout ships, had several redundant entry points, so that no one could get locked out in a strange environment.

He opened the control panel with shaking fingers, wishing he had more control over his body right now. He didn't want his team to know how nervous he was, although they could probably guess.

Maybe they would chalk it up to adrenaline. Or maybe they were just as nervous, and even more excited.

No one said anything. He could hear some ragged breathing, but that was about it.

The panel revealed a triple-coded entry, just like he expected. That calmed him. He had to type in a pattern with his fingertips. The ship would then identify him as a student in the *Brazza Two*. In the past, the ships had to confirm that someone was in the program that was going to use the ship, but so many records weren't kept up that the instructor corps abandoned that system and just put regular student records in place.

The instructors figured there were other ways to prevent students who didn't belong from getting on the ships.

And those ways were the ones that Crowe had discovered, overridden, or planned for.

He had planned for this one. The ship asked him for the class code. He'd found that about a week ago. He swept his forefinger across the flat-screen pad four times, then placed his entire hand on the screen.

Nothing happened.

Was he going to fail at this, lose this competition, because he had underestimated the access code to the ship he needed? What would Tessa say about that? She rarely teased him about his failures, but this would be too rich to ignore. She would—

Metal against metal squealed, followed by a rumble and a series of small clicks. Five of his team members stepped backwards. They had been too close to the back end of the scout ship—the end that was slowly opening like a cargo ship door.

Just like it was supposed to do.

He let out a half laugh, catching it before it became an exclamation of joy. Still, he couldn't keep the smile off his face as he nodded to his team.

He gave a one-finger symbol—index finger up—and then pointed at the dark interior. He stepped into the darkness first, even though a captain never went first. But he wasn't a real captain (yet) so screw it.

He wanted to run, but he knew better than that. Instead, his boots caught on the ramp, making banging sounds as he walked up it.

Lights came on around him the deeper he went into the ship.

His team—his *crew*—flanked him. Once they were all inside, he nodded at Maida, who would be his second in command on this journey. She grinned at him, her round face and green eyes filled with joy. He had picked Maida for this one because her scores on all of the tests they had done in the simulation were the closest to his.

She was the only other person who had managed each test along the way. Everyone else had failed at least one.

She walked over to the interior control panel for the door and the environmental system, and pressed it, shutting the cargo door and making sure the environment was suited for the team. Proper oxygen mix, proper temperature, full gravity.

Still, they would grab environmental suits as they passed through the armory on their way to the tiny bridge. In a couple of the simulations, things had gone so badly awry that the fake crew needed environmental suits.

Even though those simulations were outliers, they happened. And Crowe was cautious enough to prepare for the worst and hope that it would never come to pass.

He glanced at the crew. They were smiling at him, the nerves gone—so far as he could tell. Maybe the crew was all excited about this part of the mission.

In his estimation, this was the most dangerous part to them and their future careers with the Fleet. If they got caught at this moment, without having achieved their objectives, they'd join all the ignominious previous students who had tried to get a ship out of the docking bay.

Those students often lied about the reason they were leaving. Most of them were fleeing the school.

Crowe wasn't, and he figured he would have the simulations to back him up, but he still hated this part.

He led his crew out of the cargo area and into that narrow armory. The armory was empty; it wouldn't be stocked with weaponry unless the scout ship was going off on its own for real. But environmental suits had to remain with all ships at all times.

Still, he felt a thread of relief when he opened the uniform storage and found dozens of suits in various sizes hanging from pegs, just like they were supposed to be.

Apparently he hadn't entirely believed that the suits would be here.

Everyone grabbed a suit, then spent a few uncomfortable minutes sliding it on over their clothes. Crowe's suit was newer than the suit he had in his dorm room, and it took him a moment to figure out that the suit operated by touch-command. He left the hood down, and the gravity in his boots off.

He didn't wait for anyone else as he headed to the tiny bridge.

The *Br2 Scout3* was a midrange scout ship—or so its specs said—designed for regional exploration. The *Br2 Scout3*'s standard crew could expect to be on board for weeks, maybe months, as the exploration went on.

That meant there were two levels on the ship—operations and residential. He wasn't interested in residential; the crew wouldn't be on board that long. But operations had to have a fully functional engineering section, weaponry and defensive capabilities, and a bridge big enough to handle a minimal crew which, Fleet regulations stated, was five people at one time.

The bridge was on the opposite side of the ship from the cargo bay. So he jogged in that direction, a little surprised at the time it took. The simulation estimate for that seemed to be wildly off.

Of course, the simulation didn't take into account the equipment left in corridors from the *Br2 Scout3*'s last mission, or the way that the sharp angles of the *Br2 Scout3*'s design slowed down anyone scurrying across the ship.

The *Br2 Scout3* was just barely small enough for a crew of ten to run it, although crew compliment said that this ship needed a minimum of thirty, should the ship be gone for longer than a day or two.

Crowe finally reached the bridge, and was relieved to find the doors open. He had planned for four minutes of struggle with the control panel so that his crew could get into the bridge. He wouldn't need those four minutes, which was a good thing, since he had already wasted them and a few more getting to the bridge.

He wondered how Tessa was doing. He hadn't heard any sirens or notification of a lockdown, and he would have, since the *Br2 Scout3* was still on board the *Brazza Two*.

So she hadn't been caught.

The others of his crew joined him, environmental hoods down, looking a little flustered and sweaty from their own jogs across the ship. Maida reached his side.

"Ready?" she asked in a tone that told him she thought he was having second thoughts. If one word could sound like a shove in the back, that *ready* was it.

"Yep," he said, and stepped inside the bridge.

He had expected something small, but not something this claustrophobic. The ceiling was low, the lights old and a bit grey, the way that lights from a century ago were made. The bridge was designed like half of a bowl, with everything leading to the lower level down front. That level included a wide variety of screens, which could be toggled together to form a holographic representation of space itself.

He had thought that sounded exciting when he first found out about the design of this type of scout ship. He thought the bridge would seem vast. But now it seemed a little cheap, and the downward dip just looked like a hazard rather than a design feature.

Maybe that was because of the equipment. The equipment had been updated, but it looked grafted on, like a bandage over a particularly ugly wound.

The consoles were too large, for one thing, all of them a little too square for the design. The captain's chair, standard in larger ships, had been removed here. In fact, in order to make room for the extra equipment, every single chair in the bridge was gone.

He felt a little dizzy and then realized he'd been holding his breath. Not that it mattered. He hadn't tested with modern up-to-date equipment. His simulation had been based on the older ship, the design that *Br2 Scout3* had been built to, not the one it had been upgraded to.

"Wow," Adil said from beside him. "This thing has an *anacapa* drive."

He was looking at the *anacapa* container, near the navigation controls.

Crowe cursed under his breath. He didn't want to be anywhere near an *anacapa* drive. He thought he had picked a ship without one.

He'd studied the drives enough to know they were unpredictable, and the last thing he wanted was one of his people messing with one, and getting them all in trouble.

"We're not touching it," Crowe said. "In fact, we're not even opening the container. The first thing I'm going to do when I get to the controls is lock us out of the *anacapa*."

"No need," Maida said. "None of us want to touch it, right, gang?"

The entire crew chorused their unwillingness to touch the *anacapa* drive. He felt some of the tension leave.

This was why he had picked the ten people that he had. They believed in the same things he did. And they had that risk-taking attitude that he liked. Only they weren't reckless in their risk-taking. They took *calculated* risks.

"All right," he said. "I'm holding you guys to that, mostly because we're behind schedule as it is. Stations, everyone."

They all had assigned places and tasks. Navigation, shields (should they be necessary), and, most importantly, at least to him, recording the mission, not just on the ship's system, but on separate systems.

The crew was heading out to see a Scrapheap for the first—and maybe only—time in their lives. They needed a record of the visit.

"Here we go," he said.

And they all descended on the bridge, ready for the challenge of a lifetime.

Be the first to know!

Just sign up for the Kristine Kathryn Rusch newsletter,
and keep up with the latest news, releases
and so much more—even the occasional giveaway.

So, what are you waiting for?
To sign up go to kristinekathrynrusch.com.

But wait! There's more. Sign up for the WMG
Publishing newsletter, too, and get the latest news
and releases from all of the WMG authors and lines,
including Kristine Grayson, Kris Nelscott, Dean
Wesley Smith, *Fiction River: An Original Anthology
Magazine, Pulphouse Fiction Magazine, Smith's
Monthly,* and so much more.

To sign up, go to wmgpublishing.com.

ABOUT THE AUTHOR

New York Times bestselling author Kristine Kathryn Rusch writes in almost every genre. Generally, she uses her real name (Rusch) for most of her writing. Under that name, she publishes bestselling science fiction and fantasy, award-winning mysteries, acclaimed mainstream fiction, controversial nonfiction, and the occasional romance. Her novels have made bestseller lists around the world and her short fiction has appeared in eighteen best of the year collections. She has won more than twenty-five awards for her fiction, including the Hugo, *Le Prix Imaginales*, the *Asimov's* Readers Choice award, and the *Ellery Queen Mystery Magazine* Readers Choice Award.

To keep up with everything she does, go to kriswrites. com and sign up for her newsletter. To track her many pen names and series, see their individual websites (krisnelscott. com, kristinegrayson.com, retrievalartist.com, divingintothewreck.com, fictionriver.com, pulphousemagazine.com).

The Retrieval Artist Universe
(Reading Order)

The Disappeared

Extremes

Consequences

Buried Deep

Paloma

Recovery Man

The Recovery Man's Bargain

Duplicate Effort

The Possession of Paavo Deshin

Anniversary Day

Blowback

A Murder of Clones

Search & Recovery

The Peyti Crisis

Vigilantes

Starbase Human

Masterminds

The Impossibles

The Retrieval Artist

CPSIA information can be obtained
at www.ICGtesting.com
Printed in the USA
LVHW091545100220
646428LV00009B/126